A Dream Life

F Sur

Suraci, Patrick J.

DATE DUE			
SEP 09 2021			

A Dream Life

Patrick J. Suraci

ARCHWAY
PUBLISHING

Archway Publishing books may be ordered through booksellers or by contacting:

Archway Publishing
1663 Liberty Drive
Bloomington, IN 47403
www.archwaypublishing.com
1 (888) 242-5904

ISBN: 978-1-4808-7130-4 (sc)
ISBN: 978-1-4808-7131-1 (hc)
ISBN: 978-1-4808-7129-8 (e)

Library of Congress Control Number: 2018914716

Print information available on the last page.

Archway Publishing rev. date: 01/17/2019

To my husband, Tony Perkins

Thank you for your assistance and encouragement:

Sharon Nettles
Joe Romanaskas
Doreen Younglove
Pauline Miller
Rachel McKinney
Carroll Baker
Domingo Zapata
Linda Stasi
Jennifer and Scott Uhl
Belinda and Mike Geen
Gary Colombo
Anthony Colombo
Tony Perkins
Jan and Jeff Ware
Dr. John Provet
Thom Rivera
Dr. Jacques Hacquebord
Barbara Urbanik

ONE

A Dream Come True

As the US Army truck careened around the sharp curve at the top of the mountain, Philip Greco lurched forward, grabbing the arm of the soldier next to him. The truck shook and rattled even though the road was smooth. Philip thought, *Forget about the enemy. I'm going to have to be careful the army doesn't kill me with this lousy equipment.*

The post he was headed for was Hardt Kaserne, the former Nazi barracks that had been called the "Adolf Hitler Kaserne," in Schwäbisch Gmünd, a little town fifty kilometers from Stuttgart. Philip had been sitting in the back of the bouncing truck for two hours. The hard wooden bench pressed into his aching rear end. He looked past the canvas back flap beating up and down in the wind to the town below, and his thoughts began to wander. Tiny lights dotted the countryside and sparkled like diamonds. It looked as if the world had turned upside down and the sky, with its twinkling stars, was below the mountain.

His fear made him want to bury his head in the arm of the soldier he had just grabbed. He was alone and didn't know what the future held. He didn't even know where he was going to sleep that night. It could be a barracks with twenty guys, as it had been at Fort Dix in basic training. He knew he had to get the top bunk so it would be more difficult for a bully to pull him out. He also knew he wouldn't be able to escape the sight of guys around him exposing their penises as they masturbated during the night.

Philip remembered the words of the priest at Saint Malachy's Actors' Chapel in Manhattan. "You should tell the army psychiatrist that you're a homosexual, and then they won't take you. It will be very difficult to be with all those men in the showers and sleeping in the barracks," he had warned.

But Philip didn't want the stigma of having been rejected for homosexuality following him for the rest of his life. "I can take whatever they give me. I can do it as well as a heterosexual," he had promised the priest.

This is a far cry from my life as an actor in New York City, he thought. Living with a bunch of soldiers had been unimaginable.

With a final lurch, the truck came to a violent stop. They were finally at Hardt Kaserne. Again, Philip grabbed the arm of the soldier next to him to keep from falling off the bench.

The soldier asked, "Hey, you want to marry me?"

"I'm sorry," answered Philip.

The soldier laughed. "That's okay. I'm going to get me some fräuleins tomorrow. German girls love American cock."

Trying to fit in, Philip countered, "And I bet you have a lot of cock ... and bull for them."

"You bet I have. Here—you want to feel it?" He grabbed his crotch to show the outline of his cock.

Philip murmured, "No, thanks." He did want to touch it, but that would be too dangerous. He hadn't had sex with another man since he was drafted and started basic training at Fort Dix, though he had come close.

Philip had found the army base at Fort Dix completely disorienting, with identical barracks in straight lines. He felt like the basic certainties of life had been removed. He hadn't known where he would sleep, where he would get his gear, or what he would eat—or even if he would be able to eat it.

Not only had this new army life been unsettling; it also included an additional component of danger for Philip. In 1959, although many recruits felt the army was like prison, it actually could lead to a real prison for Philip if he expressed his homosexual desires. Sergeants and other officers were constantly on the lookout for homosexual behavior. They would court-martial participants and send them to Fort Leavenworth, a federal maximum security prison in Kansas.

Amid this terror, army officials provided the basics required for life—food, clothing, and shelter—to give the new recruits a false sense of security. Philip recognized this technique as similar to brainwashing. He had to protect himself from succumbing to that domination and maintain his individuality.

From the first day, it had been torture. Philip couldn't understand the logic of this program. It had begun with his head being shaved by a laughing barber, who quipped, "Hey, Greco, I could make a fortune selling your curly locks."

Next, he was sent to the supply clerk. Philip told the man his size, but it didn't really matter. Shirts, pants, underwear, socks, and boots were randomly thrown at him. None were his size. He had to join the other recruits who were trying to exchange clothes to get approximately their correct sizes. He was assigned to a platoon and specific barracks without any obvious method to the madness. He had nothing in common with any of the men in his platoon. They mainly talked about having no sex drive because of the saltpeter that was put in their food. This didn't seem accurate to Philip; every night he heard squeaking noises from the springs of bunks while soldiers masturbated. But he was afraid to touch himself after the sergeant's lecture threatening to cane any hand that touched any penis.

Although Fort Dix, New Jersey, wasn't far from New York, Philip might as well have been in Siberia when he had to march through snowstorms carrying twenty-five pounds of gear. The army's concern for the recruits' well-being was brought to light when one of them died of a heart attack on the march—after telling his superior officer he had heart trouble.

Philip received some support from another gay soldier, Jack. They helped each other endure their shared revulsion to the cursing, farting, vomiting, drunken straight recruits. However, no one could help on the night Philip had to stand in formation in the cold winter rain. The recruits had been "asked" to buy government bonds, and the money would be deducted from their meager soldiers' pay. One of them had refused, so the captain called out all the troops in the barracks and had them stand in the freezing rain until the lone holdout agreed to buy bonds. After four hours, at midnight, the soldier "agreed."

Philip and his bunk mate, Frankie, who was also from New York, had the same sarcastic sense of humor, and at first, they also enjoyed wrestling together. When "Fuck-Your-Buddy Week" was announced, Frankie, who claimed to be straight, pulled Philip under his blanket to wrestle and simulate intercourse to entertain the troops in their barracks. With the others unable to see, Frankie grabbed Philip's cock.

Afraid to breathe, Philip didn't say a word and sometimes ventured to touch Frankie's cock. Frankie got on top of Philip and grinded his crotch into Philip's hard erection until Philip had an orgasm and came in his regulation shorts. Philip worried he could get a dishonorable discharge—or, worse, go to prison—for homosexual activity, but at twenty-three, his sex drive was stronger than his fears.

However, Philip's friendship with Frankie ended abruptly when they were on maneuvers. To escape bullets from the hypothetical enemy, they had to crawl under barbed wire via a single hole in the wire. Philip hesitated in consideration of Frankie, who then dived right through the hole without any regard whatsoever for Philip's safety, theoretically leaving Philip to be shot.

Next came advanced training. Philip was assigned to the unit making dog tags. It was easy to operate the machine punching out the metal dog tags. However, he had to be precise in entering the correct information: the soldier's name, serial number, religion, and blood type. This was a soldier's identity card if he died in battle.

The first time he entered the dog tag shop, he was greeted by the officer in charge. Captain Brock was a round black man with a twinkle in his eye. He welcomed Philip and introduced him to the five good-looking white soldiers who were already working there. They all had blond or light hair, muscular physiques, and sparkling eyes that laughed at secret jokes. Philip felt out of place with his black curly hair, slight build, and frightened brown eyes. They seemed unusually friendly with one another and with Captain Brock. Philip was determined to be as professional as possible so as not to draw unwanted attention.

Captain Brock was friendly toward him, which was

unusual in the army. A few weeks into Philip's assignment in the shop, the captain asked Philip, "Would you like to come to my home for a party with the other guys?"

Philip didn't know how to behave with his new acquaintances, so he answered, "I have to clean my M-1." He knew not to call it a "gun" for fear of being punished.

"You're going to miss a good time. But we'll make it up next time."

"Thank you, sir."

A few weeks later, while Philip actually was cleaning his rifle at night in his barracks, he was called to the orderly room. *Oh God*, he thought, *what have I done now?* He raced to the orderly office. When he arrived, he was surprised to find Captain Brock there. The captain said there was an emergency job to make dog tags. Philip was relieved and followed him to his car.

As the captain pulled the car away, he said, "You couldn't make the party last time, so I brought the party to you." He laughed as he pulled a pint of whiskey from his jacket and turned his car in the direction of the shooting range.

"Aren't we going to the shop, sir?"

"I just said that to get you out of the barracks. We're going to the range, where we won't be disturbed." He took a swig of whiskey. "I thought you could use some relaxation. I know how hard it is to live with all those assholes in the barracks. You have to listen to all their made-up stories about getting laid." Captain Brock handed Philip the whiskey.

Philip thought he had better not insult him, so he took a little swallow. Meanwhile, Captain Brock parked the car in the dark, deserted firing range. He shifted around and put his hand on Philip's knee. Philip froze.

"You missed a good party the other night. The guys got a

little tipsy, and we played strip poker. You can imagine how it ended up. In fact, our dicks all ended up."

"I'm glad you had a good time, sir."

"You don't have to call me 'sir' here."

"Okay," muttered Philip.

"Why don't you move over here, and I'll help you relax?" said Captain Brock.

"I'm fine here, sir … I mean Brock."

"You know, I can really make you feel good. Have another drink."

Nervously, Philip put the bottle to his lips again. "You don't need me when you have all those good-looking guys in the shop. I'm really not into that, and you'd be disappointed," he said, wishing it were one of the guys from the shop coming on to him in the car.

"Well, at least let me give you a back rub."

"Okay." Philip turned around and moved closer to Captain Brock.

"Take off your shirt so I can feel your skin."

Philip didn't know what to do, so he removed his shirt and began to pray. Captain Brock's hands were smooth, and the back rub did feel good. It had been months since anyone had touched Philip's bare skin.

Captain Brock said, "You are so tense. You needed this."

After a few minutes Philip said, "Thank you. That was so good." He pulled his shirt on and moved over to the passenger side again.

Captain Brock said, "I could get you stationed here permanently for your two years. Then you could go into New York for auditions."

Immediately, Philip regretted having told the captain that he had been an actor in New York before he was drafted.

He thought it wouldn't be possible to act in a play in New York while in the army in Fort Dix. Wrestling with these thoughts, he told Captain Brock, "I was hoping to be stationed in Germany. I studied German in high school and would love to see the country. They've been sending a lot of guys there."

"They're also sending them to Korea. I could get you shipped there."

Philip gasped. "You're a nice guy. You wouldn't do something terrible like that. Please."

Captain Brock laughed. "No, I wouldn't torture you with Korea. Well, I think I'd better take you back to the barracks. You won't tell anyone about this."

Philip knew that was his trump card. Captain Brock also could be court-martialed and sent to Leavenworth prison. "No, of course not," Philip reassured him.

Two

Dream Interrupted

Staring at the massive gray cinderblock buildings enclosing the quad of Hardt Kaserne, Philip wondered how he would survive this claustrophobic prison for the next two years. The cold January wind swept him into the core of this overreaching edifice.

A sergeant barked at them to get into formation. Philip's dance training came in handy now; he was good at standing militarily erect and assuming whatever position was demanded for executing required exercises. Some of the other soldiers slouched beyond repair. Some were so muscle-bound that they could not perform squat jumps. Philip excelled at one hundred.

The sergeant growled, "All right, you smartasses. Who graduated from college and can type?"

Philip felt obligated to step forward; he knew he had to admit his academic background or be chastised when they found out. He thought about the punishment he had received in basic training for not confessing that he had a bachelor of arts degree in psychology; he had been put on latrine duty cleaning toilets and urinals. Afraid to say much, he mumbled, "I did. And I can type."

"You hit the jackpot," the sergeant guffawed.

Two other men admitted to college degrees.

The sergeant continued, "Well, for a change you're lucky. You guys go to the commanding officer." He pointed in the direction of the CO's office.

Philip and the others marched over to the office, where the commanding officer interrogated them individually as if they were murder suspects. He asked, "What college did you go to? When did you graduate? What did you think of your professors? Were you ever reprimanded for anything?" Once he was satisfied he turned them over to his second-in-command, executive officer Major Trenton. The XO's only question was "Who knows how to type?"

Philip felt trapped again. In addition to taking typing at his Catholic high school, with a nun who had charged around the room pointing her ruler at the typewriters, smacking the hands of the students who were not working fast enough, in typical army fashion he had been assigned to a typing class in advanced individual training at Fort Dix, and by the end of the eight weeks, he could really type.

After Philip revealed his ability, Major Trenton picked him to be the court-martial clerk.

Philip gulped. "I don't know shorthand, sir."

"No one does. Don't sweat it."

"What do I have to do, sir?"

"Go to the court-martial trials and write down as much as you can of what everyone says. Then you write up a report of the trial, and I'll sign it."

Philip felt terrified when he thought of the consequences of a court-martial for the accused, especially when he had to record everything in longhand. But one of the benefits of being the court-martial clerk was that he would share a private room with one other clerk, rather than being thrown into a room with ten or twenty soldiers. He would still have to use the common latrine, but he hoped he might be able to time it so that there would not be so many raucous soldiers there, when he went.

Philip was introduced to the other clerks who would work in the CO's office. One of them, Aloysius, who seemed uptight and prissy, would be his roommate, though not for long. He was planning to marry his girlfriend, who was coming over from the States, and then he would move out of the room and into an apartment in town. Philip dreamed of having the room all to himself—a luxury unheard of in the army.

Working in the office turned out to be almost pleasant. Philip hardly saw the CO and was supervised by the XO, Major Trenton, a tall, sturdy, serious black man from the Bronx. Philip wondered if the fact that they were both from New York was why Major Trenton had picked him to be his assistant.

The hours weren't bad either. During the day, if Philip had a break, he liked to walk to the wire fence at the edge of the compound and gaze at the abandoned castle on the adjacent Hohenstaufen mountain. There was a patch of grass people were permitted to use, and Philip would lie down on it and fantasize about what had gone on in the castle. Sometimes, in desperation, he even longed for basic training at Fort Dix. At least there it had been possible to go to New York when he had an overnight pass.

He and the other clerks usually finished in Major Trenton's office around five, and Philip then could go to chow before the food was gone. But after that, he had the dilemma of how to kill time for the rest of the night until lights-out. He usually went to the library and read or listened to classical music. He could also listen to original cast albums of Broadway shows. *The Sound of Music* was a popular show, so the library had that cast album. Philip's acting partner, Barbara Streisand, who later changed her name to Barbra, actually had been an usher for the show at the Lunt-Fontanne Theatre. He recalled that she once had said, "Musical comedy is the lowest form of entertainment." At that time, Philip had teased her about having to watch the show eight times a week. She had replied, "It's not so bad because there are a lot of scene changes, and it's like a movie."

In their acting class Barbra had performed a monologue she had chosen from *Medea*. She was only seventeen at the time, and the acting teacher, Eli Rill, had said, "That was pretty good, but don't you think you should play characters closer to your own age?" That did not please her.

Barbra's next assignment had been an improvisation in which she had to play a maid who had been goofing off all day and now had only fifteen minutes to set the table before her employer got home. Barbra raced stage left and returned with a tablecloth that she flung across the table at center stage. As the tablecloth cascaded to the floor on the other side of the table, she ran around to retrieve it and stumbled into the table. The class began to laugh. This infuriated her. She picked up the tablecloth and slammed it down on the table. The class laughed louder, and this unsettled her. She galloped stage right and returned with some china, which she threw onto the table, smashing a cup. The students kept laughing, and she angrily sent silverware flying to the tabletop. The class broke out in hysterical laughter, and her improvisation ended in a flurry of applause, but she was livid.

Rill said, "You have a flair for comedy."

After class she fumed, "Who does he think he is? I didn't come here to become a comedian."

Then, after several classes in which Philip received harsh criticism from Rill, he got upset.

Barbra told him, "He doesn't understand you. He is going to ruin your sensitivity. I also go to another acting class. Why don't you come there? We can do a scene together because I'm not interested in working with any of those students. I want to play a part where I have proper speech. I want to get rid of my Brooklyn accent."

Philip said, "I was in a play at home—*The Swan*. It's about a princess and a tutor. You could play the princess, with good speech. I can help you."

They went to rehearse at Barbra's apartment in the projects in Brooklyn, where she lived with her mother. There Philip had an idea. "Can we go up to the roof?"

Barbra said, "Yes. Why?"

Philip said, "You can stand on the roof and look down at all the people on the street. This can give you the sensation of being high above them and superior to them like the princess."

Barbra agreed, and they went to the roof of the building, fourteen stories high. She looked over the edge at the hundreds of people passing by. She said, "They're like ants, busy going to work and home. That is their life."

Philip said, "You live in a palace and wear silks and diamonds."

Barbra's posture was elevated, and she spoke the way she and Philip imagined royalty would speak, or at least, she spoke without a Brooklyn accent.

Afterward, Barbra's mother prepared a snack for them.

When Barbra was out of the room, her mother said, "My daughter is going to be a movie star."

Philip gasped, knowing Barbra did not have the customary movie-star look; she had long, straight dirty-blonde hair down to her waist, she wore black clothing with white makeup, and she lined her eyes and eyelashes in black. He thought her mother was expecting the wrong thing for her. He said, "She's very talented. She's a good actress on the *stage*, in the *theater*." But this did not dissuade Barbra's mother. She had a mother's instinct.

One student from class, Helene, was a professional singer in nightclubs. Another student was Susan, Barbra's best friend from high school. One evening Barbra, Susan, and Philip went to Helene's apartment on East Sixty-Third Street. While Helene was playing the piano and singing for them, Barbra asked her, "Would you please record my voice? I've never heard it on tape."

Helene said, "I'd love to." She played the piano, and Barbra sang into the recording machine.

Although Susan and Philip were accustomed to Barbra's singing and didn't think it was exceptional, Helene recognized her potential at once and told her, "You have a Sarah Vaughn quality. You should study voice."

Barbra laughed. "Oh, I just do it for myself. I would never sing in public." So Barbra left the unlabeled tape in Helene's apartment, in a big pile of unlabeled tapes.

Helene later offered that tape to Philip if he would go through the huge pile; he was in the army at that time, on leave in New York for only a couple of days. He wasn't able to find the tape, so it remained missing.

During this time, Barbra took an interest in Joe, another student from acting class, because he claimed to be able to conduct a séance. One evening Barbra, Susan, Philip, and Joe sat around a table in Philip's dark living room with the windows closed, the only light a candle burning brightly in the middle of the table. While Joe mumbled his incantations, they held hands, or rather squeezed hands out of nervousness, and they all could feel the electricity flowing from hand to hand.

As they entered into a deeper concentration, the doorbell rang, and they all screamed in shock. Philip's roommate and former girlfriend, Arloha, had forgotten her key. Philip went to the door and let her in, and when she discovered the séance in progress, she excitedly joined the circle.

Soon afterward, the candle suddenly went out, and everyone screamed again. They turned on the lights and discovered that the wick had been pushed down into the candle wax, extinguishing it, even though the windows were closed and there was no draft and no one had touched the candle. That ended the séance.

Too frightened to go home in the dark, Susan and Barbra spent the night with Philip on the sofa bed, fully clothed. Arloha had to go to work the next morning, so she slept in the bed in the next room. Afraid to fall asleep, Barbra sang every song she knew. After a while, Philip shouted, "Barbra, will you shut up and go to sleep!"

Philip's first court-martial assignment in Germany was a shock. Everyone spoke quickly, not giving a thought to his task of writing down their words in longhand. It seemed to Philip that the soldier was being judged guilty before he was even tried. His own defense counsel appeared to admit that his client was guilty. The prosecution and defense lawyers, officers at the post, were friends.

Going forward, the officers usually called Philip into the deliberation room with them after the trials. They would pronounce the soldier's guilt and then ask Philip what sentence they should impose: "Do you know him? What kind of soldier is he? Do you think he's a good guy?" Philip always spoke favorably about the defendant because he knew the defendants didn't have a chance during the trial. Sometimes the officers would consider what he said and give the defendant a lighter sentence.

During his free time, when he got a pass, he liked to escape the stress of the trials by walking down the mountain on a path that took him through the juniper trees of the Swabian-Franconian Forest and into town. The trees along the path were tall and dark, like in classical stories he had read. He thought that the poetry and artistry of literature he had studied for years came alive with the beauty of nature and were not just intellectual concepts. They blended with reality in this beautiful setting.

The path ended at a narrow cobblestone street, which led to a Roman arch. The first time Philip walked through, he felt like a knight in armor going to unknown territory during the crusades. Once he actually posed under the arch with his coat slung over his shoulders like a cape. The Marktplatz, the gathering place for the townspeople, was dominated by a statue of the Blessed Virgin, as if she were overseeing this Catholic congregation. The gingerbread buildings around the square sent warm feelings through Philip's body. He didn't feel so alone here because in an odd way he felt part of this new environment; it seemed familiar from childhood fairy tales filled with castles and gingerbread houses and cobblestone streets.

During these walks he felt that the pieces of his life were coming together, and he felt more whole than ever before.

He had heard about a place, Café Margrit, that had the most amazing pastry, and at dusk one day he wandered the streets in search of it. A teenage boy on his motor scooter stopped near him. The boy had a glowing German face, with twinkling blue eyes and blond hair. "Can I be of help?" the boy asked with a German accent.

"Oh, I'm looking for Café Margrit."

"I know where it is. I shall show you," offered the boy. "Is that correct English? I am studying in school."

"Yes, that's very good English," Philip said complimentarily.

"Can I take you on my bike? Sit here behind."

Philip climbed onto the bike behind the boy and held him around his waist. Then, not knowing the legal age here, he worried about how it would look to others, even though he had no intention of a sexual relationship. The boy was so friendly and naive that Philip could not think of approaching him sexually. In fact, Philip wished he had met someone like this when he was a boy, someone he might have fallen in love with. Now all he really wanted was a German friend with whom he could converse in German about ordinary life, not army talk. The boy sped off with a frightened soldier as his passenger, but soon the ride became a pleasant experience for Philip. He loved swaying around the curving old streets. A carefree breeze flowed over him, and he gained a sense of the simple, peaceful lives of the residents of these storybook houses.

Suddenly, the motor scooter stopped in front of a veranda with tables covered in linen and chairs upholstered in antique fabric. The windows of the building beyond the veranda glowed with soft lights, revealing tables surrounded by jovial Germans.

"Will you come in with me and have some pastry?" Philip offered.

"Yes. I would like to practice English," the boy responded politely.

"What is your name?"

"Werner. What are you called?"

"Philip. I know that the German phrase is 'Wie heissen zie?'—'What are you called?'—but it is better in English to say, 'What is your name?'"

"Thank you. That is what I want to learn—the way Americans really talk."

"Well ... you might not want to learn everything American soldiers say."

Inside the café, once he was convinced that people were not staring in concern at a fifteen-year-old boy with a twenty-three-year-old soldier, Philip relaxed. The fireplaces bounced bright beams around the room, enclosing them in a warm cocoon away from the chill of the evening. Philip was living his European dream of gemütlich company.

The pair spoke freely about their lives. Werner told Philip that his father had died and he and his mother had to earn a living. He dreamed of going to America to make a lot of money so that his mother could have a new life. "Will you come home to meet my mother?" he asked innocently.

"What will your mother think?"

"She will like you. She likes that Americans are in Germany to keep the Russians away."

Philip did want to meet Werner's mother but was worried that she might question his motivation in befriending her teenage son. He would have to be content with this chance encounter.

On one of Philip's forays into town, he discovered an unusual café. It did not look at all like a typical *gasthaus*. In fact, it looked like what Philip imagined a café in Paris to be. It had a small bar and small cocktail tables with plush chairs. The walls were filled with modern paintings. A rug covered the floor and gave a warm feeling to the room. Soft lighting and classical music completed the scene. There were no screaming, drunken soldiers, only soft-spoken customers who appeared to be real Germans. Philip sat at the bar because he wanted to speak with the bartender, a handsome, blond, friendly man. Philip learned that his name was Hans and he owned the bar. Hans must have sensed that Philip was attracted to him because he subtly flirted with the soldier.

After that, Philip tried to get a pass at least once a week to go to the bar. One night, he said to Hans, "I have an overnight pass. Do you know a hotel where I can get a room?"

Hans whispered, "You can stay at my apartment. But you must wait until I am ready to close the bar and then leave. Go across the street and wait for me. Don't let anyone see you."

Philip was ecstatic. When closing time arrived, he followed Hans's instructions and waited anxiously in a doorway across the deserted street. Finally, Hans appeared at the door and locked up the bar. Philip crossed the street to join him, and they walked to Hans's small second-floor apartment in silence.

As soon as they were inside and Hans had locked the door, Hans said, "I always take a bath after work. Do you want to join me?"

For a long time Philip had hoped for something like this, and once in the bathtub, he immediately became hard. He played with Hans's penis, but it remained flaccid. Philip wasn't too upset, thinking it would be different when they got into bed.

It wasn't. *My beautiful, impotent dud,* thought Philip. *The joke's on me.* He had fantasized about Hans for months. Excitement and anticipation had filled him every time he had gone to the bar. Now he had nothing to look forward to. His fantasy was over, and he would simply have to deal with reality. But he could still hope to find someone with whom he could have a real relationship.

THREE

A Glance in the Canteen

Philip's college friends from Canada, Ann and Trudy, miraculously appeared at the entrance to the post one day. Philip and the girls hugged each other and practically cried. Never had he imagined having a visitor. How could anyone gain entry into this heavily guarded fort? He didn't even know if there was a procedure for such an unheard-of occurrence. Philip couldn't just walk freely off the post but had to have a formal pass signed by his commanding officer, granting him permission to leave the base, and he had to return at the prescribed time or face real prison. How could Ann and Trudy, from his past life, be in this prison of his present life?

He thought back to his college days. In the 1950s, "good girls" did not have sex until they married. At Philip's Catholic college, the girls had even lived in the convent with the nuns. The boys had to brave the rigid face of Sister Gemma to pick up their dates and had to return them untouched before midnight. The boys might get a good-night kiss at the door of the convent, if they were lucky.

"How did you get here?" he asked in astonishment. "Where did you come from?"

"Greece," deadpanned Ann.

"Greece! Did the men rape you?" kidded Philip.

"They tried, but we're too smart and too strong for them."

"How did you get here?" Philip asked again.

"We took a taxi from the village," said Trudy.

Exasperated, Philip screamed, "How did you get on the post? I don't even know if a civilian has ever come here before!"

"Oh," Ann said. "We're going to be working at the PX in Stuttgart. Our boss called your commanding officer and got permission for us to visit you. So we took the train from Stuttgart to Schwäbisch Gmünd and then got a taxi. And here we are!"

"How did you get the job? You're not even American."

"Well, Canada is not the enemy," laughed Trudy. "We know someone who is a friend of the officer in charge of the PX, and he helped us get interviews. I guess they were glad to get college grads to work in the PX. We start next week."

"We also wanted to see if you were really in the army. You look so funny in that uniform." Ann looked serious.

Philip responded, "What did you think I'd be wearing?"

"You always had stylish clothes," exclaimed Ann.

"I'm so happy to see you. I'm sorry if I sounded stunned," Philip said. "Let's go to the canteen. You can have real American food."

"A real American hamburger?" shouted Ann.

"Hamburgers are one of the benefits of being in the army," Philip said.

It felt so homey and comfy to have friends from his past

visiting him here on this bleak army base in Germany. Philip felt truly content for the first time in a long time.

As they walked into the canteen, a sea of khaki and testosterone washed over them. Noise bounced from wall to wall. All eyes focused on the girls—all except one pair of eyes, belonging to a soldier who was in the middle of telling a joke to his laughing buddies. Philip was drawn to his sparkling eyes. He couldn't imagine anyone being so happy while in the confines of the army base. He glanced over the soldier's body, hoping the man wouldn't notice him staring, and admired the way the army fatigues clung to that beautiful trim physique. Everyone else faded into a mist as Philip stood there transfixed. He shot an arrow of desire at the soldier while all the other soldiers were aiming arrows of longing at the females. The energy in the air almost knocked him over.

"Where do we order?" Ann asked.

Philip forced himself back to reality as he pointed to the counter. "What do you want? I'll get it."

Ann stated, "A real hamburger, rare, with lettuce and tomatoes, and french fries."

Judy said, "I'll have a hamburger too. But I want mine well-done. No fries, but I'd like onion rings."

Hoping he could remember their orders, he walked as close as possible to the strange soldier on his way to the counter.

Philip couldn't stop looking at him. He didn't care anymore if the soldier saw him staring, but the soldier, wrapped in laughter and conversation, was oblivious. Philip tried to see the color of his eyes but was unable to because of a radiant glow around him. Philip knew only that he had to meet him.

Philip and the girls had to sit at a crowded table, which meant that the girls relished both their burgers and the attention of the male soldiers sitting with them. Philip continued to look at this intriguing soldier. The girls' voices faded into the background.

He noticed the strange soldier making a clicking sound with his tongue, evoking more laughter from his buddies. He was removing his front tooth from its bridge and snapping it back into place. His face wasn't perfect. He had what one would call a Roman nose, with a slight bump that didn't really look like a bump when you faced him. How was Philip going to meet him? He didn't know any of the soldiers with him.

Suddenly, the alarm rang, and all the soldiers jumped. It was the signal for them to go to the field. In case of a real attack, this was how it would begin.

Philip said, "I have to go."

"But you haven't finished your hamburger!" exclaimed Anne.

"It doesn't matter," Philip said. "We have to go on maneuvers."

"What's that?" Trudy asked.

"We go into the forest and play war games," he explained. "You'll have to find your own way off the post." As Philip rushed toward the door, he bumped into his dream soldier. "I'm sorry," Philip blurted. "My friends don't understand what we are doing."

"I don't understand what we're doing!" the soldier laughed.

"You're right," Philip agreed. "What barracks are you heading for?"

"Number 1."

"I'm in number 2."

"Why don't you get your gear, and I'll watch it while you get your friends off the base."

"That would be great." Philip knew he wasn't going to help

the girls, but he would do anything to see this soldier again. "I'm Philip Greco, the court-martial clerk."

"I won't hold it against you. I'm John Fitzgerald."

The sound of his voice reverberated in Philip's head, creating a dizzy feeling similar to what he'd felt while crossing the Atlantic Ocean to come to this moment in his life. He lunged for John's hand as if it would save him from drowning.

Now Philip was excited to go to the field, knowing John would be there. He ran to his barracks to grab his war gear. Once outside, he told John that he didn't have time for the girls but had to find the CO's jeep. He ran in between two rows of roaring, dust-filled trucks and yelling soldiers who were scrambling to find their vehicles in the chaos.

"Get your ass in the jeep!"

Philip jumped into the seat next to the CO, who asked, "Greco, did you bring your typewriter?"

"No, sir. I'm sorry. I forgot. I'll go to the office and get it."

"Never mind. It's too late now. Jenkins! Go get it and ride with the chief warrant officer. We'll meet you in the field."

The jeep sped out of the quad toward the field. *How strange that the typewriter is my main weapon of defense,* Philip thought. *What will be the consequences of forgetting it?* Philip felt as if he lived on the edge, never knowing what would come next, benevolence or malevolence.

In the field all the battalions worked together. All the troops pulled guard duty. So he was able to ask the XO if he could pull guard duty with John Fitzgerald. He got his wish, but it was also the graveyard shift—0400 hours until 0800 hours.

John seemed not to mind the early hours. He told Philip, "It gives me a chance to get away from the animals I have to work with."

Everyone in the camp was asleep. John and Philip took turns lying in the damp grass to get a few minutes of sleep while the other one manned the machine gun and was alert to detect an approaching enemy.

John was at the machine gun, with Philip lying near him, when he said, "We have to be careful not to get caught sleeping. And you better not lie so close to me. I got in trouble on the post on a recreation day. There was a large hammock, so Jenkins and I both got in it. It was fun swinging back and forth and rolling over on each other. The XO caught us and ordered us out of it. He said that only one person at a time was allowed; two people might cause an incident and give others the wrong idea, and you wouldn't want to pay the price for that. We knew that he was talking about homosexuality."

Philip asked, "You know Jenkins?"

Hesitating a little, John replied, "We used to hang out a lot until he told me he loved me. He wanted to have sex with me. I asked him about his wife, and he said that she knew about him with men. She overlooked that because she wanted to be married to him. I told him that I didn't feel the same way about him. I liked him as a friend but was not attracted to him sexually. That caused a rift in the friendship, and we drifted apart."

When it was Philip's turn to sit behind the machine gun, he said, "My ass hurts. These branches are sharp. Let's clear them out and put some soft leaves here. My ass is sensitive."

"We have to keep it in good condition. You never know what you might need it for," laughed John.

"I know," joked Philip. "I'm sitting on a gold mine with these horny soldiers."

"Being with only men for so long, it does become tempting," chuckled John.

Philip wondered if this was really a joke. He had no idea what John's desires or experiences were. Maybe it was only usual army humor. For Philip it wasn't. He had desired John from the first time he saw him in the canteen.

Being on maneuvers for a week was not so bad for Philip because he was in the CO's tent, with all the amenities. John was not so fortunate. He had to maintain the howitzers with all their dirt and grime and had to sleep in a tent near them with five other soldiers. But at least John was put on a list to go into town to have a shower every three days.

Philip was also on the shower list, but twice when his name came up, the CO said he needed him to type an important document. After being bounced from a shower twice, Philip refused to go into town when the CO finally said he could. Everyone was shocked, knowing how fastidious he was. Philip explained to John that he was not going to let them get the best of him. He would refuse a shower for the whole seven days they would be in the field. The CO was furious but felt it would not be prudent to order him to take a shower.

Philip and John had a pleasant moment in the sun on a day when they had a few hours' break. Philip had been assigned to clean the CO's jeep, and John came over to his area to help. When they had finished cleaning the jeep, Philip gave a bottle of beer to John as a reward. They sat in the open jeep, with the relaxing rays of the sun pouring down on them, and talked.

John asked, "What did you do before you got trapped here with these animals? You seem different from them."

"Where should I start?" questioned Philip.

"From the beginning. Where were you born?"

"In upstate New York. We lived in an Italian ghetto. Practically everyone on the street was related to me. I didn't realize we were so poor until I went to high school. Our neighborhood was so safe. We felt we belonged there. Do you know that feeling?"

"Yes, and I know I didn't have it very often. What happened in high school?"

"I went to a Catholic boys' high school. There were a lot of rich kids. They had their own cliques. And the football players were the gods on campus. They even imported players, and we had our own stadium. We were too good to play with the public high schools in the city and only played out-of-town prep schools. I wanted to be friends with some of the players but didn't dare approach them. There was one boy they called Bubbles; they said it was because he was always blowing bubbles, but the rumor was he was really blowing them. I never found out if it was true, but Bubbles didn't seem to mind. He went along with their teasing in the hallways at school."

"God, I didn't have any sex in high school. Did you?"

"Only with one person," replied Philip, intentionally not revealing that it had been with a male. This guy had happened to be the big stud on campus, with all the girls after him, so no one had suspected.

"What did you do after high school?" continued John.

"I got a scholarship, so I was able to go away to college. I couldn't wait to get out of that town. I was liberated in college. I became a real person. The first year, we had to live in the dorm, so that taught me how to be independent and stand up for what I believed."

"Did you graduate?"

"Yes. Got a BA in psychology. Did you go to college?"

John grimaced and said, "For one year. I dropped out because I wanted to be an artist. The only course that was helpful was the History of Art. My parents freaked out. My mother dreamed of me becoming a doctor or lawyer. My father was the opposite—a construction guy who got rich. He resented me for doing what I loved. He thought the army would 'make a man' of me."

"What did you do after you dropped out of college?"

"I painted beautiful scenery. I was brought up in California, so I loved the ocean and the beaches. Eventually, I took art classes. I kept in touch with a couple of girls from college. I dated them, but it didn't work out."

Philip felt an arrow pierce his heart. John was three years younger and had gone out with only girls, it seemed. He probably did not have any experiences with men. Philip had dated girls in college, but there had been no sexual activity with them. His sexual activity had been strictly with men, but it had been sex without love.

Philip asked, "What do you plan to do when we get discharged?"

"I'd like to travel around Europe to the museums to see all the great paintings. Then I think I'll go back to California to paint. I like living there. What about you?"

"I studied acting in New York with a director from the Actors Studio. Barbra Streisand was in my class. Maybe you've heard of her—she's beginning to make it. I have to go back to New York and try to get a job acting. It's so hard. I hope I don't lose my motivation to be on Broadway."

"I think you'll do it. You seem to be a very determined person. I'd like to paint you. You have beautiful wavy black hair."

Philip, overcome, replied, "Really? There are better-looking guys on the post."

"I see something different in you," John said. "You have a sad depth in your eyes. It makes me want to comfort you."

"I have been sad for a long time, over my sister Loreen. She has schizophrenia, and everything my family does revolves around her—we always have to consider what her reaction will be."

"I know how you feel. My mother had a breakdown and was in the hospital for a long time when I was growing up," John confided. "I was so afraid they would keep her away from me. She was the only one in my family that I felt close to. My brothers were jocks, and my father wanted me to be like them."

Philip said, "I used to hate gym. I was always the last one picked. I was embarrassed because I wasn't good at sports."

"My mother is the only one who appreciates my paintings. She is sensitive and cultured, from her convent school days. We correspond regularly, but the only thing I've had from my father was a greeting card with sandpaper on it that said, 'Rough, isn't it!'"

"That's a shame."

John reminisced, "I used to go to the library to look at art books. I love Van Gogh."

Philip agreed. "Me too. The Rijksmuseum in Amsterdam has a huge collection of his paintings."

John said, "I'd like to see them."

"So would I."

"We're lucky to be stationed here. We can travel around Europe."

Philip said, "I haven't had a chance to go anywhere."

"You should start planning."

"I don't have anyone to go with."

John offered, "Hey, I could go with you."

Philip beamed. "That would be great. Sometimes I feel so scared that no one will ever understand me."

"I've been scared too—to show my emotions," John said.

"Why?"

"Afraid to get rejected."

Philip said, "You seem to be happy most of the time."

"I try to have a positive outlook," John explained. "When I'm sad, I don't show it."

"I don't show my emotions because I'm afraid no one will be interested," Philip said.

"I think you're an interesting person."

"Thanks! Do you really think so? You're so good-looking. I bet the girls were after you."

"I did have a lot of girlfriends. But something was always missing."

Philip understood. "I know what you mean."

John said, "Hey, I meant it when I said I would like to paint you. Do you think we could find a quiet place away from the drunken animals?"

"I would love that," Philip said. "When we get back to the base, I'll ask the CO if we could use the office after hours."

"I can't wait."

FOUR

A Message from Angels

After the maneuvers in the field, Philip and John returned to the post. They began to go to their special hideaway, Café Margrit. Although they were the only soldiers there, they blended into the atmosphere of happy friends enjoying mouthwatering desserts and aromatic coffee. The café was always filled with well-dressed and well-mannered Germans. Only once in a while did they spot an American or Englishman. Very few tourists came to Schwäbisch Gmünd, although it was well known for its gold and silver artisans.

Philip and John had no desire to engage the other patrons in conversation. They wanted to be alone in the midst of this beautiful crowd of gentlemen and ladies. The warm glow of candles filled the inside of the café.

John confided in him, "When I get out of the army, I would like to finish college."

Philip nodded. "I think you should."

"I'm afraid that I won't be able to get through college. What if I flunk out?"

Philip said, "I can tell that you have a high IQ and would be able to finish college."

They wanted to keep their haven a secret, so the only army people they took to the café were George and Philomena, a married couple who had welcomed them into their home and had become family. They were simple and straightforward but also had a New York City edge, having grown up on Long Island. Because they were a heterosexual married couple, they were allowed to live in town and have a car. A single man or a homosexual couple could not even dream of such a possibility.

George said, "Philip, Philomena told me that you have friends from college living in Stuttgart. I could drive us there sometime."

Philip happily replied, "Yes, there are two girls I went to school with who're working in the PX. We were very close in college, and it's great to have them over here. I think you'll like them, and I would like John to meet them."

Philomena added, "Oh yes, arrange it, Philip. We can go practically anytime that's good for the girls."

"I want to hear the real stories about Philip in college from them," John said, intimating some juicy stories might be told.

Philomena beamed. "Yes, yes, I want to hear all about it."

Philip sighed. "Okay, but first I have to go to Paris. You all have gone, so I'll have to go alone. There are a couple of French girls—identical twins—who spent a summer in my hometown. We've been writing, and they're waiting for me to come. They want to show me the real Paris."

John said, "I would go with you, but I don't have any more leave time."

Philip said, "That's all right. I'll be okay as long as I have Parisians to help me."

In the taxi on the way back to the post, John said, "I wish I didn't have to go back to my barracks with the animals."

"When Aloysius gets married, I'll ask the captain if you can move into my room," Philip said.

"That would be great. I promise I won't be such a slob. I'll keep everything according to regulations, so we'll always pass inspection."

"It would be great to have you there."

But when Aloysius got married, the captain said no one could move into the room until another clerk was assigned; the new clerk would have to move into Philip's room. So Philip was the only one living in the room when it was time for him to go to Paris.

Philip had always dreamed of going to Paris. Fulfilling this dream almost made it worthwhile to be in the army. The twins, Yvette and Brigitte, met him at the train station, Gare du Nord. They had grown more beautiful and even more difficult to tell apart. They were happy to speak nonstop in English.

It was twilight when they walked down the Avenue des Champs-Élysées. Heads spun at the sight of the trio, with Philip in the middle and a dazzling identical twin on each side. They took him to a local restaurant they frequented. The owner rushed over to kiss them and made a fuss over Philip, the "wonderful American soldier." A waiter scurried over to take their order. Suddenly, Yvette was gesticulating wildly and issuing orders to the waiter.

Philip had never seen her this way before and was alarmed. He asked, "Is everything okay? You seem upset."

"No," laughed Yvette. "I was just ordering the bread."

If this was the French way, Philip decided, he was happy to let her order for him. The food was delicious and lived up to his expectations.

After dinner Yvette and Brigitte took him to La Cave to see Apache dancers. They walked down a stairway to a club that seemed to be carved out of a real cave. The only French he could understand from the crowd was the occasional mention of Sartre or Truffaut, names he knew from his reading and from the movies. He felt at home with these Bohemian people and wished that John were there with him. Their table was at the edge of the dance floor. When the dancers came out onto the floor, they were fierce. The man grabbed the woman by her hair and spun her around on the floor. Then he threw her with such force that she landed on their table. Philip jumped up to help the woman, but she rushed into the arms of her partner. During this dance of love, the man and the woman took turns beating each other.

When the dancing was over, Philip told the girls about his mother, who had been a ballerina. "During one of her performances, she did an Apache dance. As the dance requires, my mother and the male dancer took turns attacking each other. When her partner threw her on the floor, my father jumped onto the stage and punched him. This was a favorite family story that my father always vehemently denied. But it did seem a bit suspicious that my mother had to give up dancing after that episode, as a prerequisite for my father to marry her."

The next day the girls had to work, so Philip was on his own. He went to the Louvre Museum and the Eiffel Tower and then enjoyed being a tourist, sitting outdoors at Les Deux Magots café in Saint-Germain-des-Prés. With his dark hair and German clothes, he did not look like a typical American, so he was able to listen in on conversations that the English-speaking travelers had no idea he would understand.

At the next table were two American men. One said, referring to Philip, "He's so cute. I'd like to say something to him."

The other said, "Go ahead."

The first man said, "I don't know French, and maybe he doesn't understand English."

Philip was flattered by their attention and enjoyed maintaining a mystery about himself. Eventually, he left, disappointing his admirer. He wandered through Paris to the Tuileries Garden, where, overcome by exhaustion from walking all over the beautiful city, he had to sit on a bench.

He watched the people pass by. Wearing his distinctive German jacket, he did blend in with the European crowd. The jacket was made of forest-green and pale-gold worsted fabric and was square-cut at the waist. So assimilated was he that a young man his age approached and said, "Wie gehts."

Philip replied, "Gut, danke; und Dir?"

The young man was so pleased that he rattled off several sentences before Philip had a chance to tell him that he was American and spoke only a little German.

"I am Dieter."

"I'm Philip."

"Are you on vacation?"

"Yes. A short vacation. I'm in the army in Schwäbisch Gmünd."

"I know Gmünd. I live in Stuttgart. What are you doing for the remainder of the day?"

"I only have today and tomorrow, and then I must return to Germany. I would like to buy my mother a dress. She would love a real Parisian dress. We live in a small town, and they don't have clothes like these."

"I know a shop. My mother told me to buy her a scarf from it. I don't remember the name, but if I see it, I shall remember. It is on Boulevard des Capucines."

And Dieter did find the exclusive dress shop. The sales-ladies fluttered around them when they learned that Philip was going to buy something for his mother. The women asked if any of them were about the size of his mother. He picked out the smallest saleswoman and a black wool dress he liked. She offered to try it on for him. He was so grateful. The dress fit her perfectly, and the woman seemed to be the same size as his tiny mother. All the other salesgirls loved it and thought it would be the perfect Parisian dress for America. Dieter agreed, so John purchased it and had them ship it to his mother. It would be the most expensive dress she'd ever had.

Dieter asked Philip, "Do you have plans for dinner?"

Philip said, "I would like to have plans with you."

Dieter replied, "That is what I want."

They strolled down the boulevard until they saw a small shop similar to an American deli. The cooks were roasting chickens on the sidewalk in front of the shop. The mouth-watering smell convinced them to buy a chicken and take it back to Philip's room. They also bought french fries and other side dishes to make a complete meal. It started to rain, so they covered their heads with newspapers and laughed all the way to the Hotel Du Pantheon in Saint-Germain-des-Prés, a modest hotel that the twins had recommended. It was on the Left Bank, which was where Philip had wanted to stay.

As soon as they got to Philip's room, they removed their shirts, shoes, and socks and, hesitantly, their pants. They toweled off and hung their clothes to dry. The room was compact but had a desk, a chair, a chifforobe, and a bed. They spread their feast on the bed and then sat opposite each other in their underwear, to enjoy the most delicious chicken they'd ever had. They reveled in their newfound friendship, telling each other about their lives. Although they came from very different backgrounds, they had a good rapport. There also was a sexual tension between them.

Philip wanted to reach across the food to touch Dieter. His blond curls called out to be touched, and his blue eyes had an inviting look. But Philip was paralyzed. What if Dieter wasn't interested? He didn't want to ruin a pleasant day with him. Later, when he thought about it, he realized that Dieter also had attempted to indicate his desire for Philip, but the difference in cultures had prevented that message from being conveyed.

Dieter said, "I would like to stay the night here, but I came with friends. They would worry if I did not return tonight."

Philip said, with a tremor in his voice, "I understand."

"I could stay with you tomorrow if you like."

Philip beamed. "Oh yes, I would like."

Dieter said, "I am happy. I should return to my hotel now."

As they both put on their clothes, which had dried, Dieter admired Philip's belt. Philip eagerly gave it to him.

Dieter thanked him. "You must take my belt. Now we are tied to each other until tomorrow."

"That's beautiful," Philip responded.

They embraced, and Dieter left. Philip felt an empty space in his chest. He also felt guilty when he thought about John. He didn't have any commitment to John, yet he felt like he was cheating on him. Imagining what it would be like with Dieter tomorrow, he drifted off to sleep.

He awoke with a start and looked at the clock. It was

5:00 a.m. A terrible dread washed over him. *I have to get back to the post,* he thought. He couldn't explain what was happening, but he started packing furiously. He went to the front desk to leave notes explaining his departure to Dieter and the girls. The clerk was surprised that he was leaving so suddenly, a day early. Philip asked him to call a taxi to take him to the station, so that he could get a train to Stuttgart. He would take the very next train after he arrived at the station.

All the way back to the base, on the trains to Stuttgart and then to Schwäbisch Gmünd, he prayed that he would arrive in time—in time for what, he didn't know, but he felt a sense of urgency and impending doom.

He arrived in time for John to tell him that there were to be changes in the sleeping quarters. There was an elaborate plan that made no sense to the soldiers, but like inmates in a prison, they had to obey or be punished.

The CO had decided he didn't need another clerk, so the captain was going to assign an artilleryman to Philip's room. Philip knew the guy and had a good relationship with him. So he asked the artilleryman if he would mind going to another room so that John could move in with him. The soldier readily agreed, since he knew what "good buddies" Philip and John were.

John asked, "What made you come back early?"

Philip said, "I think my guardian angel sent a message."

FIVE

Moving for Life

The day John moved into Philip's room was an ordinary day on the post, but it was an extraordinary day for them. A married couple moving into their first home would probably be as excited as they were, but Philip and John would never experience exactly that married moment of joy, since that was denied to homosexuals.

Philip could only compare his own excitement to a time when he was in college. As editor of the yearbook, he had been in charge of the publication party; it was the only way to thank his editorial staff, who had worked tirelessly for little praise and no money. After the party, clutching the yearbook, he had paused in front of the dorm and looked up at the full moon. He had wanted to fully enjoy this special moment of complete contentment; he knew it was a feeling that might never come again. His prognostication was correct: the very next day, he had learned that his only sister, Loreen, had had a schizophrenic break, and her condition would haunt him for the rest of his life.

However, at this moment he felt only ecstasy over John's

moving in. The room held regulation furniture—two bunks with footlockers, two high wardrobe closets, and a stationary radiator beneath the window—complemented by John's record player. He had received permission from Sergeant Davis to keep it, if he kept it as clean as the rest of the room. Philip knew there was not much choice when it came to redecorating the assigned pieces of furniture, but just having John's duffel bag on the bunk opposite his was a welcome addition.

John had brought a bottle of scotch too, so that they could celebrate. The bottom of his wardrobe was a good place to stash it. He hummed as he arranged his gear in his footlocker according to army regulations. Philip offered to help, but John's adrenaline was pumping, and he needed no help. He was setting up residence as if they would live there for a hundred years—just the two of them against an army of brutes.

John had brought his favorite records by Mario Lanza and Dean Martin. Philip thought Mario Lanza's *The Student Prince* was apropos, since the University of Heidelberg was not too far away, but Dean Martin! He was surprised that John was passionate about him, but that night he would discover why.

Philip had two good friends across the hall—Sheldon, an intellectual New York Jew, and Jeremiah, a Louisiana philosopher. He invited them to share dinner at the mess hall so they could meet John. As they stood in line, John motioned toward the other soldiers. "I don't want to breathe the same air that they breathe," he said, apparently feeling relief that he could be different and still exist in the army with his friends.

The four of them had a celebratory supper that night. It was the chef's specialty, SOS, commonly referred to as "shit on a shingle"—something indescribable substituting for mashed-up hamburger and faux cream sauce soaked into a piece of stale toast leftover from breakfast. They planned to go into town another night to celebrate with real food.

Philip and John's first night together seemed comfy and safe, as if they had bunked together forever. Philip knew that he desired more physical contact with John, but he was content to be alone with him in the same room. The horrors and fears of the army disappeared. He forgot for that night that he was being held captive by army rules and regulations.

He said, "You're free to do whatever you want in our room, even if we have to break our backs to put it back together for inspection."

John replied, "What I really want to do is paint your portrait. I feel we have the perfect environment for it now. I couldn't paint in peace at home. My father was always making disparaging comments. My mother tried, but she couldn't stand up to him. He had my brothers, the jocks, on his side, and I was the odd man out. I don't feel that way with you."

For the first time since they had been in the army, they both felt comfortable in their own bunks.

Sleepily, John said, "Now you'll see why I love Dean Martin." He played the record:

> Stars shining bright above you
> Night breezes seem to whisper, "I love you"
> Bird singing in the sycamore tree
> Dream a little dream of me.
> Say nighty-night and kiss me
> Just hold me tight and tell me you'll miss me
> While I'm alone and blue as can be
> Dream a little dream of me.

Philip's heart floated across the space between their bunks

and sank into John. Never had Philip experienced this with anyone else. He prayed that John was saying these words to him. He also prayed that this moment of paradise would last a little while.

The next morning, Philip awoke with a smile. Was he still in the army? This feeling was uncharacteristic. He looked over to the other bunk and knew why he felt this way.

"Good morning," chimed John.

"Morning? I haven't heard that in a long time," said Philip.

"'Good morning' or my beautiful voice?" questioned John.

"Come on. You know what I mean," laughed Philip.

They hurriedly threw on their fatigues and ran to the quad for morning exercises. This time the cold didn't bother Philip. He hit the ground next to John and started push-ups with an intensity rivaling that of an Olympian athlete. He couldn't believe the brightness surrounding him. His love for John made the most mundane things take on a heightened sense of reality.

Philip sailed through the routine waves of duties, humming all the while, as the CO ran in and out of the office, throwing work at him. The CO finally asked if he was high. Philip realized that he had to tone down his feelings before they aroused suspicion and gossip, a favorite pastime of army personnel. After work, John related his experience of also actually enjoying work on the howitzer that day. They laughed and said it must have been the power of Dean Martin's singing.

That gave Philip an idea. After supper he told John, "I'm going to the library to pick up something. I'll meet you back in the room."

John seemed perplexed but went along to the barracks.

When Philip returned, John anxiously asked, "What is it?" He was dying to know what Philip had been up to.

Philip said, "You will have to wait until bedtime."

Then Sheldon and Jeremiah arrived to play poker. John had difficulty concentrating on the game, preoccupied with curiosity about Philip's secret. He was gazing into the distance when it was his turn.

"What are you doing?" Sheldon asked John.

"I'm sorry. I wasn't thinking."

"You're all dreamy. Are you in love?"

"Yeah, sure. With the army. I might even re-up for another four years."

Jeremiah asked, "Why don't you give us a shot of whiskey?"

"Sure," replied Philip, grateful for the distraction. He went over to the wardrobe and got John's bottle of scotch. Sheldon and Jeremiah were already prepared, having brought their canteen cups.

"How do you guys get away with it?" remarked Jeremiah.

"I give some to Sergeant Davis," answered Philip. "He's really an alcoholic, so he'll do anything for a drink."

"This is great. Keep giving it to him. Do you think I could do it?" questioned Jeremiah.

"You better not, or he might catch on. If you want to buy a bottle, we'll keep it here, and you can come over anytime you want."

"Okay, that's a deal."

They wrapped up the game before lights-out so that Philip and John could have some time to themselves. Philip wondered if they knew how he felt about John.

"Now tell me," pleaded John, referring to Philip's afternoon secret.

"Okay. Do you know the Broadway show *Carousel*?"

"No, but I've heard about the movie."

"I got the record from the library. Let's get into bed, and I'll play it for you. Please listen to the words."

When he heard the overture, John said that he liked the score. Then when the singing began, he was silent. Philip could hear him breathing as they absorbed the music. Philip willed the message to be sent to John when Julie sang:

If I loved you,
time and again
I would try to say all I'd want you to know.
If I loved you,
words wouldn't come
in an easy way.
Round in circles I'd go,
longing to tell you but afraid and shy ...

"That is beautiful," said John.

"Yes," said Philip. He wondered if John could understand that that was how Philip felt. John was becoming the focus of his life. Until he had joined the army, a major part of Philip's life had been consumed by his parents and his mentally ill sister. Now he had someone of his own to love.

They were together every moment when they were free. Only their military duties could keep them apart. John had guard duty, walking the perimeter of the post in eternally freezing weather once a week. Then sometimes he had KP, kitchen patrol, where grease permeated his being. Philip had guard duty also, but it was in the comfort of the CO's office every two weeks. He also had KP, limited to peeling potatoes in case the CO needed him on a moment's notice. It was not acceptable for him to smell of grease. Sergeant Walker's red face filled with rage at this limitation on his sadistic powers.

John's tasks left him physically exhausted, while Philip's duties produced psychological stress. One of Philip's main goals was to prove to Executive Officer Trenton, who was black, that he was not prejudiced. It was common among the troops to express prejudice toward black soldiers. Sometimes comments were made in jest to evoke laughter, but often the slurs were sincere and produced fighting. Whenever Philip witnessed such behavior, he felt it was his duty, as the court-martial clerk, to intervene. Most soldiers were careful in their treatment of Philip. They knew how easily they could be court-martialed and that if they were, they would need his help.

A test of Philip's acceptance occurred when he had guard duty with Major Trenton. They would sit in the office in shifts, guarding the records and the payroll. Trenton, a New Yorker, was sensitive to the discrimination he had encountered there before enlisting in the army. He was not about to endure that behavior now that he was a major.

Major Trenton had a private bedroom off the office to be used when he was on guard duty—a striking example of his privilege. When he invited Philip to use his bed when he had a break, this marked the undeniable friendship between the two.

One night he asked Philip to sit beside him on his bed. Then he took his cigarette out of his mouth and offered it to Philip. Philip did not miss a beat; he accepted the cigarette and stuck it in his mouth. Trenton was married and had two children, and Philip did not detect any sexual intent. Trenton was fond of Philip but couldn't show it; an officer could not treat an enlisted man as his equal. To express his gratitude, he engaged in small gestures of kindness, hoping Philip would understand the full import.

Over the next three months, when Philip and John were confined to the post, they went to the movies and sometimes even to the beer hall with Sheldon and Jeremiah. When they got a pass, they went to eat at some of the best restaurants because American dollars were worth so much more than German marks. Their favorite restaurant served *Ungarisches gulasch* and oxtail soup. They shopped for clothes and antiques. They walked the quaint cobblestone streets. They sat in the Marktplatz, the town square, and practiced their German with the students there. Of course, their special romantic place was Café Margrit, where they drooled over *Apfelstrudel mit schlag*—apple strudel with whipped cream— and looked silently into each other's eyes.

One night they had gone to a gasthaus to have typical German bratwurst and cabbage and plenty of beer. Upon returning to the post, they heard the siren signaling them to go to the field. Philip, fortunately, was assigned to the CO's office, but John still belonged to the howitzer battalion and had to drive a truck for them. His sergeant wasn't concerned about the wisdom of having John drive after he had been drinking. Trucks and howitzers were roaring out of the post, leaving a wall of dust in their wake. Sirens were blasting, and drunken soldiers were running around, trying to secure their gear. The chaos was an accurate simulation of war. The frenzy was contagious, resulting in soldiers shouting and scrambling to get their M-1 rifles while hoping they would not accidentally shoot someone.

Philip, worried about John, went to his truck to see his warrior off to battle. Their heads were close together.

"I'd die for you, Philly," exclaimed John.

"Just live for me, Johnny," replied Philip, actually fearing something dreadful would happen to him. Their words were more intimate than the kiss they might have shared were it not forbidden.

Philip counted the long ensuing hours as he listened to garbled walkie-talkie communications from the field. Executive Officer Trenton had told Philip to wake him if anything happened and had then retreated to his bedroom.

Unfortunately, Philip's premonition came true. Over the squawk box came a tired voice saying that one of the trucks had turned over while going down a hill. It appeared that the brakes had failed. The driver was John Fitzgerald. Philip ran to Trenton and woke him. He stammered that Fitzgerald had been injured. When Trenton pressed him for more relevant information to give the CO, Philip was able to tell him about the truck.

More news came in—John had been taken to the hospital in Stuttgart. That meant he was seriously injured. Philip tried not to panic and asked Trenton if he could call the hospital to inquire about John's condition.

"He's your bunk mate, isn't he?" Trenton asked knowingly.

"Yes, sir," Philip answered formally.

"Okay, go ahead and call. I hope it's not serious."

John nervously dialed. "This is the Seventh Artillery calling about Private Fitzgerald."

He was told that John was in the operating room, and there was no report yet. He could call back in an hour. It was late, and Philip was tired from their drinking escapade. However, he was not leaving the office for anything, except a short trip to the bathroom.

Once he was alone, he burst into tears. "Dear God, please let him live. I'll do anything you want. I'll go to Mass and confession. I'll tell the chaplain about us. Anything! But please let him be okay."

After pacing around the office for the remainder of the hour, trying to look busy, Philip called the hospital. He learned that the brakes had indeed failed, and John had broken his leg when the truck crashed at the bottom of a hill. The main thing was that John had a clean break, and it would heal completely. He would have to stay in the hospital for about a week.

During that week Philip was in agony because he was not allowed to go to Stuttgart to see John. In fact, his CO became suspicious of Philip's desperate wish to see John, who only had a broken leg.

At last John returned. The pair was invited to dinner at the apartment of Philip's close friends Philomena and George, who made a sumptuous dinner to celebrate John's return. They encouraged Philip and John to drink the special wine they had bought for the occasion. After a couple of hours, John announced he was going to be sick. Philip quickly helped him to the bathroom, which was in the hall outside the apartment.

Knowing they could not be heard, John said, "I'm not sick. I have to tell you something."

"What?" Philip asked nervously.

"I don't know how it happened."

"What happened? You can tell me," begged Philip.

John whispered, "I'm in love with you."

Philip said, "I'm in love with you too."

John anxiously asked, "What do we do?"

"We don't have to do anything. Don't worry. We can go on just as we are."

"Are we going to have sex?"

"If you want to. But if you don't, don't worry. We don't have to have sex. I just want to be with you."

"And I want to be with you—all the time. I always think about you."

"My whole life is you."

Tentatively, John asked, "Can I kiss you?"

"Oh yes. I'm dying to kiss you," said Philip.

They grabbed each other and kissed with the passion that had been building for months.

When they returned to Philomena and George's apartment, Philomena asked, "How are you feeling, John?"

Philip answered for him. "He's okay, just a little tipsy. I should probably take him home."

As soon as they entered their room back at the post, their love exploded. They tore each other's clothes off and landed on Philip's bed. John lay on top of Philip, sucking the breath out of him. His penis touched Philip's and grew hard. Philip guided John's penis in between his legs to that sensitive spot below his testicles. John instinctively thrust into Philip. They kissed and thrust until they both climaxed and sperm spewed between them. Then John got up, put on his army-issued white undershorts, and got into his bed.

In the morning he asked Philip, "Did we do something last night?"

"Why?"

"My shorts are on backward."

"We made love. Do you remember?"

John was silent. Now Philip worried about what John was feeling. Philip was terrified of what might happen to them now. They both went to their jobs without saying another word.

After supper, back in their room, Philip asked, "Do you still want to go to Garmisch? We can cancel our leave if you want."

"No. I want to go to Garmisch," John said.

Philip nodded and wondered what would happen next, when they went on leave to Garmisch the next day.

SIX

On Leave in Garmisch

The black night seemed endless as the train wended its way through the forests of Bavaria. Philip and John had taken the local train from Schwäbisch Gmünd to Stuttgart, then the main train to Munich, and now they had fifty miles to travel on another local train to Garmisch. The countryside rushed by them, but looking out the windows in the dark did not help them figure out where they were.

Although Philip hated the winter and the cold, this was the only time he and John could get a leave simultaneously for their first trip alone. They had chosen Garmisch, a beautiful resort town where American military personnel received discounts. It was now a recreation center—a far cry from a Nazi military hospital center, which was what it had been during World War II. It seemed fitting that the US Army should turn it into something beautiful after the war.

Philip attempted light conversation, but John had not been very talkative after their sexual activity two nights ago. He appeared to be deep in thought, though he seemed quite comfortable sinking into the cushioned train seat across from

Philip, and from time to time, Philip caught John glancing at him.

When they reached Garmisch and descended the steps of the train, darkness and cold enveloped them. There were taxis waiting at the train station, so they knew they wouldn't freeze to death getting to the hotel. That was a wonderful thing about Germany: Mercedes taxis welcomed them in every small town.

Soon they were rushing into the warm, inviting General Patton Hotel. The fireplaces roared, and the maître d' quickly sat them at a table and called over a waiter. Being familiar with American soldiers, the waiter said, "We have a specialty I think you will like—melted cheese on toasted German bread, the most delicious cheese. It is from Bavaria."

Philip and John nodded and also ordered *Weissenbier* with a slice of lime. When the food arrived, they didn't know if it was the power of suggestion or the reality of Bavaria, but it was indeed "the most delicious cheese."

They sat as close as possible, with their legs touching under the table, which was covered with a long cloth. Philip could feel the warmth not only on his body but also in his heart. They ordered additional portions of the melted cheese, until they could eat no more. Then they waddled down the long narrow corridor to their room. They stripped and lay on the feather duvet, luxuriating in the R&R.

Giggling, they rolled into a ball, wrapped up in each other. Philip began a downward path of kissing John's body. When he got to John's penis, he gently kissed it.

John jumped up. "No, not that!"

"What do you want to do?" Philip asked, stunned.

"Kissing is enough," demanded John, although he had an erection.

"I can't stop there. I want to make love to you. Look at your hard-on!" asserted Philip.

"I can't do it now."

Philip got up and put on his clothes. "I'm going to the bar. Maybe I'll pick up someone."

When he got to the bar, he was relieved that he could sit at a small table in a corner and hide. He was still shaky when he ordered a beer. Staring into space, he tried to figure out what was going on with John. He worried that John had had sex with him that first time in their room only because he was drunk. John must have had a blackout, because he really didn't remember it the next morning. This was a bad sign. He knew that John loved him but was confused about the complexity of their sexual contact. Lost in his thoughts, Philip didn't immediately notice that another soldier had approached him and was talking.

"I'm sorry. I didn't hear you," Philip said apologetically as he looked up.

"Can I join you?"

"Sure. Have a seat," said Philip to this handsome, muscular, grinning soldier.

"Is this your first time here?"

"Yes, my buddy and I heard about this place."

"Where is your buddy?" asked the soldier, putting an emphasis on the word *buddy.*

"He's in the room. He didn't want to come to the bar."

"Did you have an argument?"

"Something like that."

"Well, you could solve that by coming to my room."

"To have a drink?"

"We could do that and see what happens. I've been here

before, and it can be a lot of fun, especially when there's a group of us. It's a great way to relax."

"What do you mean?"

"Come to my room, and I'll show you."

Before Philip could answer, John appeared at his side. "Come back to the room," John pleaded.

Philip turned toward the soldier and said, "I'm sorry. I have to go."

"Are you sure?" asked the seductive soldier.

"Yes, we're together."

"Maybe next time," insisted the soldier.

When they got back to their room, John removed his clothes and resumed his position on the bed. "Come here. Do it," he said.

Crawling onto the bed, Philip said, "A guy in New York gave me oral sex, but I couldn't reciprocate. He told me that it was okay and not to do it until I found someone I really wanted. You're the first one I've really wanted."

Philip tentatively took John's penis in his mouth. It grew longer and harder than he had ever imagined. He easily devoured it, as if they had been doing this all their lives. It didn't matter that it was Philip's first time giving oral sex. He was so overcome with love for John that he never thought of the techniques other gay men had used on him. Although he enjoyed receiving oral sex, he had never been able to put another man's penis in his mouth. In fact, it had seemed disgusting to him. He had never been sure if this was the result of society, the church, or his own personal feelings. But not now. He devoured John's penis, which felt as if it had always belonged in his mouth.

John's moans encouraged Philip to take him deeper and

faster until John exploded into his mouth. Philip was in ecstasy. He had his hero, his warrior, his savior.

The next morning, Philip was shaving, and in the mirror he noticed John sitting on the bed, looking at him. "Don't try to make me feel guilty. I loved doing it to you," offered Philip. He was referring to Catholic guilt, since they both had been raised Catholic. He knew that John had long ago left the church, not because of his homosexuality but because he could not accept illogical tenets that he had been told to accept blindly by faith.

John opened the drapes, and the huge picture window was filled with the view of a snowcapped mountain and a tip of blue sky. It was the Zugspitze, the highest mountain in Germany. They both stood at the window in amazement. The grandeur and power of it brought them together. John said, "I read in the brochure that there is a lake and you can rent paddleboats."

"I don't know how to do that."

"I do," said John. "We did that all the time in California."

"Okay, let's go," said Philip.

Although it was winter, it was a sunny, warm, crystal-clear day. The mountain wrapped its arms around the shimmering blue lake, shielding them from cold breezes. The boats were operated with pedals. Philip had no idea what to do with them, being the quintessential New Yorker. John, who had grown up in Southern California on the water, confidently took charge and got them to the middle of the lake in no time.

It was then that Philip realized they were the only ones on the lake. He had been gazing at the beautiful mountain in front of them rather than at the water. Now he began to think about not knowing how to swim and having no life jacket, remembering that he had almost drowned in a swim class at the YMCA. He worried that what he had done to John the night before might have damaged John's psyche. He looked at John, paddling intently. Philip thought, *No one would ever know if John pushed me overboard.*

He said, "John, you know I can't swim. If the boat tipped over, I wouldn't be able to swim to shore. It would be an accident. If I drowned, I would feel content with my life. You are the only one I have ever wanted so completely." He added, "You probably could swim to shore."

John was shocked. "What do you mean? Nothing is going to happen to you." After a pause John whispered, "I loved it."

"So did I." Philip sank comfortably into the cushion on the plank in the boat. "You're not mad?" he asked hopefully.

"No."

Philip's heart soared, and he wanted to kiss John at that moment.

"I know what you want to do. It's not safe here. Wait till we get to the room. Let's go back," John said.

Philip couldn't believe what he was hearing.

After the blissful hour on the lake, they returned to their room. As soon as they were in the room, John pushed Philip onto the bed. He undressed him while taking off his own clothes and then began to give Philip oral sex. Philip was in ecstasy, tingling all over. This was not the time to try to solve the obstacles to their love. He spun around so that he could take John's penis into his mouth. Their hunger was so intense that they erupted simultaneously.

On the train going back to the post, Philip tried to decipher John's *Mona Lisa* smile. Now that they had declared their love for each other, he wondered what life would be like, living together in their private haven.

SEVEN

No Greater Love

Philip didn't have KP too often, but when he did, it was hell. He knew that he had to be the best at peeling potatoes. Sergeant Walker reigned over his kingdom of the kitchen, taking great pleasure in torturing Philip whenever he had control over him. He resented that the CO would pull Philip from KP whenever he had a document to be typed. No mere private was going to escape from the duties planned for him—peeling potatoes, scrubbing greasy cauldrons, cleaning up the kitchen. Philip was able to get through these odious tasks by pretending he was one of the witches in *Macbeth*. He scrubbed the cauldron for all he was worth, conjuring up spirits to kill Sergeant Walker.

One movie night, the kitchen was especially dirty, and those on kitchen duty were working beyond the usual time. In strode John, ready to free his damsel in distress. He dared to confront Sergeant Walker. "The movie is going to start, and Philip will miss the beginning. We've been waiting for this movie ever since we read the book. It's the only intelligent movie in months. It's a little better than *Gidget* and that ilk."

"What the hell are you talking about, Fitzgerald?" fumed Sergeant Walker.

Philip was frozen to the spot. He knew that John could be brought up on charges of insubordination and sent to the brig. This was not a free society where you could express your desires. It was a dictatorship where you obeyed the slightest desire of your superiors. He didn't want to jeopardize John's position in the battalion. Philip usually dealt with Sergeant Walker in a more diplomatic way to get him off his back.

"That's okay, Sarge. I can finish up here," Philip said, trying to mitigate the damage John had done.

Sergeant Walker's eyes were blazing. "You have a hell of a nerve busting in here, Fitzgerald. Who the fuck do you think you are? Now you're giving orders?"

"Come on, Sarge," John coaxed. "I'll make up the time tomorrow for Philip. I'll do whatever you want me to do to clean up this mess."

"All right. You're going to do whatever I say. Go ahead, take your boyfriend. He's useless anyway," conceded Sergeant Walker. "What the fuck is this special movie?"

"*From the Terrace*, with Paul Newman and Joanne Woodward. It's from the book by John O'Hara," John explained.

"Are you two supposed to be Paul Newman and Joanne Woodward?" taunted Walker.

Philip worried that in jesting Walker was coming too close to the truth. His relationship with John felt like a marriage. He was thrilled but at the same time terrified over John's brave declaration of their "friendship." There were many pairs known as "best buddies" in the battalion. They were often accused of being lovers as a means of teasing them. However, it was suspect when two soldiers did most things together and had an especially close friendship. In most cases, the buddies did not have a sexual relationship, but you couldn't be certain about all of them.

Philip wondered if the others really knew that he and John were lovers. He was always on guard to protect their secret, so John's reckless behavior frightened him—for John and for himself. He knew that some of the sergeants and other officers would love to prove that they were engaged in an illicit affair and bring them up on charges. The threat of Fort Leavenworth, the prison in Kansas for rapists and murderers, always hung over their heads like the sword of Damocles.

As they left the kitchen, Philip told John, "I want to change. My clothes smell of that grease."

"We don't have time. I love the smell of grease," teased John.

They ran to the shack that served as a movie theater and arrived just in time for the end of the opening credits. The theater was half-empty since this movie did not have as wide an appeal as *Gidget*. They found two seats together and settled down. John threw his fatigue jacket over their laps and grabbed Philip's hand.

Philip was stunned—John was not usually so demonstrative of his love. Philip was thrilled by the touch of John's flesh. Each pressed into the other's hand, attempting to convey his strong love for the other. Philip remembered holding hands out in the open with his teenage sweetheart in their neighborhood movie theater. At that time touch was enough to send him soaring into romantic feelings, as it was now with John. He felt through touching John's hand that he could flow throughout his whole body. The warmth from Philip's heart spread through his own body into his fingertips and blended into John's hand. How wonderful to love someone and to have him love you! He appreciated how rare this was.

They both felt that they could stay like this forever, or at least until the end of the movie. But that was not to be. A soldier rushed into the theater and threw himself into the seat next to Philip, gasping, "Did I miss much?"

Philip turned toward the soldier to block his view of their entangled hands under John's fatigue jacket. He surreptitiously withdrew his hand from John's and said "No," lying to shut up the soldier.

Then they focused on the movie, and after the movie they openly expressed their differences of opinion about the motivations of the characters. They blurted their ideas to each other as they exited the movie shack. Philip felt confident in differing with John and did not fear that it would diminish John's love for him. He could accept John's challenging ideas and still love him wholeheartedly.

They passed the beer hall, where it was "nickel beer night." The result of five-cent beers was soldiers puking all over the quad.

Philip remarked, "It's acceptable for them to get drunk and puke their guts out. And some of them will go back to their barracks and grab their entrenching shovels and knock one another over their heads. But it's not okay for two guys to hold hands."

John said, "That is the way most of the world is. What can we do about it?"

"Nothing," lamented Philip. "Except create our own world where we can be free to do what we want."

"As long as we don't let others see it," added John.

Philip allowed John to put his arm around his shoulders because that is what the drunken soldiers were doing. They could blend in with the crowd returning to their barracks. No one knew that their embrace was one of love and not one intended to prevent the other person from falling over.

On their way back to the barracks, Philip thought about ripping John's clothes off. He was extremely aroused by John's daring action in the kitchen and by his stimulating conversation about the movie. He was happy that John had put his arm around his shoulders so that he could press up against his body, and he hoped that this feeling of contentment would be sufficient if John was not in the mood. He had learned that John sometimes had no desire for sex or didn't want to have sex with a man—even Philip. Philip was puzzled by this because he knew that John had not touched a girl since his arrival in Germany. At these times nothing could persuade John to make love to Philip, despite his loving him, and Philip would become frustrated and lash out at John, to no avail.

As soon as they closed the door to their room, John grabbed him and kissed him from his head down to his penis, and all Philip's fears disappeared. He immediately became erect. He hung on to John so he wouldn't fall over. He pressed into John and devoured his lips. Warmth and desire spread from his lips throughout his body and steadily increased until he was on fire. He pulled John over to his bunk before he exploded sperm all over his pants. The fleeting thought that the door was not locked passed quickly. He would think of something to say if the sergeant came in for bed check. Now he was engaged with his lover.

Philip lay on his back and unbuttoned his fatigues. He was grateful for the baggy regulation shorts with a wide opening. John had only to open his pants and stick his hard penis into the opening of Philip's shorts. At least they had their clothes on if someone came in. John's thrusting and Philip's

61

clenching legs placed John's penis in the couple's favorite place below Philip's testicles. This was a position that thrilled them especially, allowing full-body contact.

After their lovemaking, John surprised Philip by giving him a valentine. Philip had forgotten that it was Valentine's Day. His only connection to the holiday had been in his childhood, when he would give a valentine to a girl he had a crush on. Never had he thought of giving a valentine to a boy he had a crush on. Now he had a lover who was giving him a declaration of his love.

Philip thought of the concept of soul mates. Plato had written in *The Symposium* that according to Greek mythology, each human originally had four arms, four legs, and a head with two faces, one looking ahead and one looking behind. Then Zeus, afraid of the great powers humans were developing, split them in half. Humans were then destined to search the world to find their other half, in order to become whole.

Philip had found his other half, and they fit into each other like a coin that had been cut in half with jagged edges, now blending into a whole coin. At that moment, there was nothing else in the world that Philip desired, and John's reactions that night caused him to hope that John felt the same way.

The next day, Philip convinced John to put a hook lock on the door that only they could open from inside the room. For a few months they were able to make love in relative safety when they locked the door. Crucial to the success of this plan was remembering to unlock the door before bed check, when the sergeant came in.

Because they were together, the months flew by. They no longer suffered the boredom of the army. As Christmas approached, they went to Stuttgart with Philomena and

George to buy presents. They split up, with Philip going with Philomena to buy a present for John. They went to a jewelry store, where Philip bought a cameo ring with a Roman soldier's profile for John. As they were leaving, Philip spotted an emerald ring. Since it was his birthstone, and he hoped John might buy him one, he asked the clerk to see it. He held the emerald up to the light, and it slipped from his hand. He heard it crash on the glass counter.

The clerk immediately said, "Please stay here. I have to get the manager."

Philip and Philomena were in shock. The manager called them into his office and said he would have to send the emerald back to the factory to see what damage had been done. Philip nervously gave his identification information in Schwäbisch Gmünd.

Filled with anxiety and worry, Philip dreaded telling John what had happened. But John said calmly, "Don't worry. We'll pay for it if it takes all our future paychecks."

Philip had not expected that. Never before had anyone made such a gesture. Now he was not alone in the world.

For weeks they were able to live in the world they had created with their door securely locked. Then reality burst in one night just before they were going to make love. Sergeant Davis tried to open the door and banged on it when he couldn't. Philip rushed to the wardrobe to grab the bottle of scotch and then unlocked the door.

"What the fuck are you guys doing? Playing hide the banana?" the sergeant screamed.

"We're just having a drink, Sarge. Do you want a shot?" John answered quickly.

"Don't mind if I do. But just one. I'm still on duty."

John filled a water glass, hoping the sergeant would drink

it all. He did. Sergeant Davis could not waste any alcohol. However, he was sober enough to tell them to take down the lock.

"First thing in the morning," promised Philip.

After Sergeant Davis left, John sighed. "That was a close call!" he said.

The next day brought a close call of a different nature. Major Trenton had to preside at a court-martial at the army post in Dachau. He ordered Philip to accompany him.

"But, Major, they have court-martial clerks at the base in Dachau."

"I don't trust any of those idiots. I need you, and that's that," Major Trenton said, ending the discussion.

Philip's main concern—and John's terror—was that Captain Jones would fly the small four-seat plane. He was famous for flying high above the clouds until the engine knocked out and then gliding the plane to a landing, hopefully on land. There was an empty seat on the plane, and John asked Major Trenton if he could go with them to help. Trenton refused.

On that day—Philip couldn't help but think of it as that fateful day—the sky was cloudy, and visibility was poor. This did not present a problem for Captain Jones. In fact, he welcomed the challenge of flying through a fog. Remarkably, the takeoff was smooth, and Philip began to relax in his uncomfortable seat. But when Captain Jones was ready to land, he said, "I can't see the fucking airstrip. I know it's somewhere around here, and we're running out of fuel."

Terrified, Philip asked, "Can't you contact them with radar?"

Captain Jones laughed. "Radar! What do you think you're on, TWA?"

Philip couldn't believe what he was hearing. "You mean there is no radar? How do you guide the plane to the runway?"

"By instinct, boy. By instinct. I think it is somewhere between those mountains. Hang on. We're going through."

How fitting, thought Philip. *Dachau is where the Nazis gassed homosexuals, and now the US Army is going to kill me over Dachau. John was right to worry about me, when I just thought this would be a painful separation from him for two days.* He prayed as Captain Jones dived through the fog between the two mountains and found the airstrip.

"See? I thought it was there," boasted Captain Jones.

After they landed, Philip had only one hour to visit the Holocaust Museum in Dachau. He rushed over to the gray cinderblock building, where he was greeted by two German soldiers guarding it. He hadn't expected that.

"May I go in?" he asked.

"You only have a short time," replied one.

"That's okay. I'll only stay a few minutes," said Philip. He walked into the outer chamber, where there were artifacts and pictures of Jews who had been interred there. Then he walked into the next room, which was bare except for the many showerheads on the ceiling. This was where the victims had been not washed but gassed. Another room contained ovens. Philip was already feeling nauseated when he received a further shock—one of the German guards came in. He could imagine the guard throwing him into the oven, but the guard only announced that it was closing time.

The next day, the court-martial and the flight back to Gmünd were uneventful. Philip arrived at night and found John asleep in his undershorts. As he undressed, he hoped John would wake up. When he was down to his undershorts, he went over to John and sat on his bunk. He whispered to him, but John did not awaken. Philip was pulling the blanket up over John when Sergeant Davis burst into the room.

"What are you doing in Fitzgerald's bunk?" Sarge said accusingly.

"He's passed out. I was just covering him up."

"You better get in your bunk. I can make trouble for you. I've been watching you two. There's something going on here."

"I'm just trying to help him. He's young and not used to this way of life."

"Yeah, well, don't help him too much," warned Sergeant Davis.

The next day, Philip told John what had happened.

John said, "I was so worried about you flying with that maniac that I sat here and drank the scotch until I passed out."

"We have to rent a room in town where we can go when we get a pass. We can't make love here anymore. Sarge is out to get us. I'll ask Philomena and George if they know of a room for rent."

They were in luck. Philomena said her landlord, Anna, had a room to rent in her house on Werenwiesen Strasse. She would accept Philip and John because Philomena recommended them. Anna was a pleasant woman who had suffered through the war. Her husband had been killed in the war, but she bore no bitterness toward Americans. She told the two American soldiers that she would rather have them protecting her than have the Russians, who had pillaged and raped. Philip and John immediately rented the room. They took some clothing to keep there, but the most important thing was a new record player. They also had a hot plate, so they could cook. And although the bathroom was in the hall, there was a bathtub; they hadn't had a bath in a long time.

Their first night was to be a feast. They bought bratwurst

and beans to cook in the pots Anna gave them. While the food was cooking, they played their new record—Rachmaninoff's *Concerto No. 2 in C Minor*. They started kissing and couldn't resist making love until the smell of burnt food caused them to jump out of bed. They realized they could make love here with no repercussions, except for the need to buy Frau Anna a new pot.

Everything was in place for as wonderful a life as was possible in the army. Philip thought about what Charles Dickens had written in *A Tale of Two Cities*: "It was the best of times, it was the worst of times." The worst of times was over for now, and soon they could begin the best of times by going on vacation in Italy in a couple of months.

EIGHT

Fourth of July, Army-Style

It was the Fourth of July, Independence Day. Philip wondered what independence they had.

On the post, the focus was America's independence from England. The army showed its loyalty to America by having a picnic; for a few hours at least, the soldiers might feel independent and actually believe that someone did care about their independence. They could even leave the post to go across the road to an open field where several tents had been erected.

Philip and John had no interest in the festivities, but everyone was ordered to go. In fact, half of the platoon had been recruited to work at the various tents, cooking hot dogs and hamburgers, distributing sodas, and scooping out potato salad (which they had made while on KP). Those men had reasons to be not so enthusiastic about the celebration.

But there were some who relished the party—the children. All the army families with children lived off-post and had to bring their children up the mountain to the field. Although parents were complaining, the children were joyous. John thought that made it all worthwhile. Philip was still not so convinced.

The kids laughed and screamed in delight at the make-shift merry-go-round. They played tag, scampering all over everyone. They played potato-sack games, racing and winning prizes. Some of them fell and skinned their knees while jumping around in the potato sacks. The post doctor and a couple of military aides manned a first-aid tent, where they provided basic treatment for the kids' minor injuries.

The sun was shining brightly, and Philip and John lay in the grass and daydreamed of the beautiful beaches they would go to on the French Riviera. For a few moments, not having to obey any ridiculous rules, they actually felt relieved, and they planned to escape this charade as soon as they could. When everyone was caught up in the merriment, they edged toward the road. Slowly, they performed the maneuvers they had learned in reconnaissance. They crossed the road without being noticed and ran across the quad to their barracks.

No one was in the barracks, so they went to their room to have a nap. Once they were inside, John unexpectedly closed the door to their room and placed Philip against it. He kissed him and ground his crotch into him. If someone tried to come in, they could move away from the door, fully clothed. They could make up an excuse about having come in for a drink.

Philip was overwhelmed by John's renewed passion, and he felt every cell in his body vibrating. He tried to merge with every cell in John's body. He became aroused not because of lustful thoughts or feelings, but because his penis was just another appendage inflamed with the love they shared. He felt complete and peaceful in John's arms, in spite of the chaos outside on the base. They kissed desperately, and Philip almost immediately came into his shorts, with John following soon after. They quickly changed their clothes and plopped onto their separate bunks to take that nap.

No sooner had they closed their eyes than someone did come bursting into the room. Sheldon, their friend from across the hall, sputtered, "Philip, the CO is furious and wants you in the office immediately!"

Philip and John were filled with dread at this ominous pronouncement and jumped up from their cots. John asked, "Do you want me to come with you?"

"It's better if you don't," reasoned Philip. "He'll just wonder why you are with me. I'll let you know what it's about."

"Okay, but let me know as soon as possible. I'll wait here with Sheldon."

⁜

"Where have you been?" the CO yelled in what sounded to Philip like an accusing tone of voice. "Never mind. Get at your desk and type up the charges."

"Yes, sir," Philip robotically responded. "What charges?"

"Rape and maybe murder."

"What—who—how did it happen?"

"Private David Smith raped a child."

Philip's stomach dropped. He clung to his desk for support. He didn't want to hear the details that he was going to have to type in the charges for the court-martial. It couldn't be true. David was the face of the innocent all-American soldier, with blue eyes and blond hair. He was even known as "the sweet soldier" in his howitzer battalion. He was not rough and crude like the other soldiers in his unit.

Recently, David had confided in Philip after being humiliated in a very public way. David said, "You're the only one I can tell what happened. You're not like the other soldiers. I know you'll understand."

Philip tried to recall all the intimate details that David had told him. A few weeks earlier David had gone with Lucas, a black twenty-year-old from Houston, and Mark, a white twenty-one-year-old from Chicago, to a whorehouse. It was common knowledge on the base that David was a virgin. He said that back home his girlfriend could not "go all the way" with him because she would have been branded a whore. Now he was anxious to lose his virginity.

David had related, "In the taxi Lucas said, 'You're going to love it. There are five girls, and they know the ropes.'"

David said that he felt uneasy when they arrived at a run-down house with shutters covering all the windows and a madam welcoming them as if they were her familiar customers.

He continued, "Lucas told the madam, 'We brought a virgin.' Then she yelled for Marlene, a beautiful, slim, young girl who took my hand and led me upstairs."

Philip vividly remembered that David had told him, "The room was shabby and smelled of the bratwurst that had recently been cooked on the hot plate. The bed was rumpled, and I began to worry about germs from previous customers. I stood by the bed as she removed my shoes, pants, and shorts. She grabbed my dick and stuck it in her mouth. I was surprised and didn't know what to do. So I tried to kiss her. She wouldn't let me. I didn't know if I was allowed to touch her breasts. I was so confused that I couldn't get an erection. Marlene pulled me down on the bed and said, 'I make it hard.' She yanked it and sucked it and tried to stick it in her vagina, but it was too soft.

"Then I jumped up and dressed as fast as I could. I told

her I was sorry and ran out of the room. She came running after me.

"'You have to pay!' she shouted as we entered the main room, where the madam and the other soldiers waited. 'Not my fault no fuckee!'

"I gave her the money. She and the others laughed."

David told them he would take a taxi back to the post as he ran out in embarrassment.

Philip assured David that it would be impossible for him to get an erection under those circumstances.

But there was more to come. A week later, David had told Philip about an incident that had just happened.

He said, "I was taking a shower when Lucas, Mark, and three other punks walked in. They all stripped and looked me over.

"'Hey, sweet soldier,' called one. 'Do you want to have some fun?'

"I answered, 'No thanks. I'm getting ready for guard duty.'

"But they surrounded me and began to touch me. Two of the slimy punks got on either side of me and began to pinch my nipples, while another put his hand on my dick. The fifth one blew into my ear and sucked on my neck. Lucas ran his huge erection over my buttocks and pressed against my rectum.

"I tightened my ass and tried to laugh it off. I said, 'Okay, guys, you had your fun. Now I have to go, or they are going to come looking for me for guard duty.'

"They laughed louder and said, 'No one is going to come in here in the middle of the night!' The soldier stroking my dick said, 'This little guy is getting hard. He wants to play. Are you afraid you'll enjoy it?'

"Lucas, still behind me, pressed harder. 'Hey, guys, I can't get in. I'm too big. Hutchins, you have the smallest dick. You go first and open him up.'

"They all rushed around behind me, except the one squeezing my dick. When he was sure that none of the others could see him, he stuck it in his mouth, but only for a second. Then he too went around to my rear.

"Hutchins was ready. 'I'm going to hurt this motherfucker.'

"Just then the door to the bathroom flew open and Sarge walked in. The five soldiers jumped away from me. 'Stop horsing around, you guys. Smith, what are you still doing here? You get dressed and be on guard in five minutes.'

"'Yes, Sarge,' I said. I was grateful to be rescued.

"'Why don't you guys leave the fairy alone before you get into trouble?' Sarge asked.

"'We were just teasing him the way we do everybody, Sarge,' Lucas said. 'He was playing along with us.'

"I didn't dare to contradict them, so I said, 'Yeah, Sarge. I'm going now.'"

When David had revealed the attempted rape, Philip was horrified at what the guys had done to him. He was at a loss for words. He assured David that he would help him figure out what to do about this harassment. To everyone else David Smith had seemed to still be the good-natured soldier he always had been—until he raped the child.

"Start typing up the charges," bellowed the CO, bringing Philip back to the present. "I told you, Smith is charged with rape, and if the child dies, it will be murder. We'll hang the son of a bitch."

How could David do such a thing? thought Philip.

As the witnesses from David's barracks entered the office and were questioned, Philip typed the story. Smith had arrived at the barracks covered in blood. When someone asked him what had happened, he said, "I got my first cherry. I'm no longer a virgin." He lay calmly on his bunk as the military police ran in. They had learned from the child's father what had happened. They grabbed Smith and punched him in the stomach until he collapsed. Then they dragged him over to the jail cell on the post.

Smith had been playing with the children at the picnic. There was one little girl who resembled him, with her blue eyes and curly blonde hair. Her father agreed to let Smith give her a piggyback ride. The child giggled with delight as she rode around the picnic grounds on Smith's back. The father glanced away for a second and then discovered that his daughter was gone.

Smith had taken the girl into the supply tent because no one was there. He raped her as he held his hand over her mouth. Then he ran out of the tent.

The child screamed for her father, who ran into the tent just in time for her to collapse into his arms. He shouted for the medics, and they came running. The little girl's injuries were beyond the expertise of the post clinic's doctor; she would have to be taken to Stuttgart for treatment. The medics placed her into the post's ambulance as carefully and as quickly as they could and sped away, leaving her parents behind.

Philip could hardly breathe as he typed the details into the charge of rape.

Chaos had broken out in the office. The child's father had been brought in to tell what had happened, and other officers had brought in soldiers who had been in the vicinity of Smith and the child on the picnic grounds.

The CO called the hospital in Stuttgart to find out the child's condition. Hanging up, he announced, "She's still in surgery. They don't know if she's going to make it." Every five minutes, he repeated the call. Enraged, he left the office to go to the officers' club for a drink.

The other officers hovered over Philip, telling him to look up the charges for murder. When the CO came into the office and announced that the child had died, the officers seemed almost happy that the charge would be murder.

Tears poured from Philip's eyes as he typed the court-martial orders. He tried to comfort the little girl's father, but of course, there was no way he could be comforted.

Philip handed the orders to the CO and escaped from the office. He wasn't sure if he had hallucinated the reactions of the officers. Could they be so heartless as to want the child to die so that David could be punished more severely? He ran to his room to tell John what had happened.

John, knowing the officers involved, assured Philip that he wasn't crazy. "And," he added, "they would do the same thing to us for loving each other, if we were caught."

Philip knew that David Smith would be found guilty, without any mitigating circumstances. He'd be sent to the US Penitentiary, Leavenworth, where he would be raped and killed by the other inmates.

And that was exactly what happened.

NINE

Italia Conquers All

After the trauma of the little girl's rape and murder, Philip and John were grateful to be able to leave the army base and go to Italy for a vacation.

They were exhilarated when their train pulled into Stazione Termini in Rome, with its cacophony of voices and jumble of colorful signs. Although Philip and John didn't have a hotel reservation, they weren't worried as they were swept along by the exuberant crowd. Soon an *Informazione* booth loomed before them, and they inquired about a place to stay. The clerk understood Philip's homemade Italian with a Sicilian twist, which he had learned from his family, and recommended a *pensione* that was clean and reasonably priced.

When they arrived at the boardinghouse, a rotund padrone, Maria, welcomed them and assured them that she would take care of them. They had found their Italian mama. It didn't matter that their room was dark and looked out on an alley. Across the way were colorful buildings with real Italians hanging out their laundry.

Philip and John loved the room and made themselves at

home. John was anxious to go to the Colosseum. He had avidly studied the history of this vast amphitheater, which had been built by the Flavian dynasty between AD 70 and 80 and had been a place where life and death depended on a whim, a thumbs-up or a thumbs-down. John had long dreamed of seeing it in person. Philip agreed to make it the first tourist attraction they visited, even though he would have preferred to go to the Villa Borghese.

Maria told them how to take the subway directly to the Colosseum. As they walked up the stairs to exit the subway, they were startled to see the Colosseum framed in the huge glass windows, looking as if it were floating in midair.

They wandered through every corridor and archway, remarking that the ancient ruins were works of art. They were captivated by the hundreds of cats living there, who apparently survived on little dishes of pasta that women brought for them every day.

Philip had a sensation of having been in the Colosseum before, which came as a surprise. His family was quite Americanized, and he had never felt so Italian in his life. John, an Irishman, had no such affiliation and was more interested in historical details. They both were filled with awe at the glory of the Colosseum.

That night they went to the Café de Paris on the Via Veneto, and it was exactly as portrayed in the film *La Dolce Vita*. A beautiful blonde-haired woman stopped traffic to get out of her car right in front of the café, and they halfway expected her to be Anita Ekberg. The carnival-like atmosphere lifted their spirits. It was fun to sit at the sidewalk café and watch people from all over the world strolling by, wearing every conceivable kind of garb.

Philip went inside to use the toilet, navigating around

many tables of joyful people. On his way back, he stopped at the food counter. It all looked so delicious that he couldn't choose just one thing, so the waiters had him taste every dish. They watched his reactions and were pleased that he loved everything.

For twenty minutes, John sat alone at the table outside. He couldn't imagine what had happened to Philip, so he went inside to find him. "What are you doing?" John asked.

"These wonderful waiters wanted me to taste everything."

"Am I going to eat anything?" John pleaded.

"Of course. Let's go back to our table, and they'll bring the food to us."

Once they were at their table, a line of waiters brought them a variety of mouthwatering dishes. They overheard the people at the next table complaining that they couldn't get a waiter at all. Those people turned out to be the Irish ambassador and his wife.

"Why are they making a fuss over us? Do they think we're someone? The Irish ambassador can't even get service," John said.

"I think they know that we're in love. The Italians die for love. Haven't you seen any Italian operas?"

"This is really like being in an opera. I've never seen anything like this place except in the movie. I wasn't sure if Fellini made it all up."

When they couldn't eat another teaspoon of gelato, they decided it was the perfect time to go to the Fontana di Trevi. They jumped into a taxi and sped down the Via Veneto. They drove down a narrow, dark cobblestone street, and as they turned a corner, the huge fountain rose up before them. They were spellbound.

"It really is something, isn't it?" Philip said.

"More magnificent than in the history books," added John.

They held hands and walked down the steps to the edge of the fountain. They sat on the railing, exchanging smiles with many other couples.

Philip said, "You know that we have to throw a coin in the fountain, so that we will return to Rome."

"Yes, and I know that you have to throw it backward over your shoulder."

Simultaneously, each of them threw a lira into the fountain. They hugged and kissed each other on both cheeks, as the Italian men did. They felt free to behave as they wished without having to censor themselves as they would in America or on the army base.

The next day was devoted to Piazza Di Spagna and the Spanish Steps, a favorite tourist attraction. It was said that, as with Times Square, if you sat on the steps long enough, you would meet someone you knew. In the blazing sun they climbed the 135 steps to the church, Trinita dei Monti. When they went inside, the cool air revived them. The frescoes on the dome were overpowering. They walked around, admiring frescoes, paintings, and sculptures. One painting was by a student of Michelangelo. John was especially interested in the different styles.

Walking down the steps was easier than climbing them had been, but the sun was still blazing. They went to the "Ugly Boat" fountain at the bottom of the steps and instinctively sat on the inside rim of the pool, where they took off their shoes and socks to bathe their feet in the cool water. It was blissful. No one chastised them, but later they learned that it was forbidden to put one's feet in the pool.

After a few minutes they put their socks and shoes back on and continued their exploration. To the right of the steps was the house where Milton and Shelley had lived. As they entered, they felt as if they were stepping back into history. On the other side of the steps was another tribute to England—Babington's Tea Room. There they had scones and clotted cream and basked in modern English customs. They couldn't help staring longingly into each other's eyes. Although most of the patrons were English and American, Philip and John did not feel inhibited by them, nor were they frowned upon.

They enjoyed visiting the shops on the Via Condotti, where the salespeople were gracious to them, even though they knew these American military men couldn't afford to buy anything. When it started to rain, they ducked into a doorway. In the doorway next to them, a lovely woman wearing a rose-petal skullcap peered out to see if the rain had stopped, and she smiled at them. It was Audrey Hepburn.

Philip grabbed John's arm. "Are we in her movie *A Roman Holiday*?"

John laughed, "She does look exactly as she did in the movie. Audrey Hepburn has a face I would love to paint."

"We'll buy a photograph of her and if you could capture her impish quality it would be wonderful."

As they walked back to the pensione on the Via del Corso, they passed a shop called John, which was probably named after Saint John. In the window were beautiful men's shoes. John said, "I've always wanted a pair of Italian shoes. They have the most supple leather."

Philip had never paid much attention to shoes, even though his father was a shoe repairman. His father had never educated him about the art of shoemaking, but if his father had remained in Reggio Calabria, he would have become a shoemaker, he had told Philip, because he had been an apprentice to a master. However, he had moved to America with his parents when he was twelve and had become a shoe repairman instead. This had proved to be a sufficient profession to support a family with the basic necessities of life.

"Do you think we will have enough money for the rest of the trip?" asked Philip, who was worried because the shoes looked as if they were handmade and expensive.

"We'll cut down on other things."

Cut down on other things, thought Philip. *Sure, my things. He cares more about those shoes than about me. I want to go to Florence and Venice.* Aloud he said, "I don't know how much we'll need for the rest of the trip."

"Don't worry," said John. "We'll find a way. We still have some cigarettes to sell."

Thank God for the army PX—American cigarettes were very cheap and were highly valued by the Italians. Earlier in the day, they had used them to barter with the carriage driver whose beautiful horse had then drawn their carriage along the Via Appia to the catacombs. On the way the driver had stopped to take them into a church that had a slab of white marble set into the floor. There were two footprints on the slab, and the driver claimed they had been made by Jesus as he was climbing the path to the Mount of Olives to be crucified. Philip and John didn't know if this was true, but willful suspension of disbelief created a spiritual atmosphere. They had thanked the driver and continued on to the catacombs.

Philip had clung to John as they went underground to the narrow dark passages where the early Christians were buried. Philip felt claustrophobic, so John put his arms around his shoulders and assured him that they would be all right. Philip put his trust in John. No one else was there. At the exit he cried, not because he had survived it, but because John had been so caring and understanding.

Now John was paying for the shoes with the money they had made by loaning money to soldiers around the end of each month. Many soldiers ran out of money before their payday at the beginning of the next month. There was an unwritten rule that if you loaned money, you got paid double at the next payday. Drinking and whoring were the downfall of the soldiers who could not manage their money.

When the couple got back to their room, John showed his gratitude by kissing Philip. All the anger and jealousy drained from Philip's body when John made love to him. He encouraged John to wear his new shoes the next day, when they would board the train for Florence.

They were filled with excitement on the way to Florence, mainly because they would see the statue of David. With the aid of Informazione, they found a pensione, dropped their suitcases, and walked to the Galleria dell'Accademia. In the corridor leading to the main salon were several incomplete statues started by Michelangelo. The figures that emerged from the blocks of marble were already works of art.

John said, "I like them just the way they are—like men being born."

Philip replied, "They are hypnotic."

When they reached the main room, where the statue of David stood on a pedestal in the middle of the room, Philip's legs gave way, and he grabbed John.

"You see! Didn't I tell you?" laughed John. "It is incredible. He carved it out of a damaged piece of Carrara marble nineteen feet high. *David* is actually seventeen feet tall. There is a power emanating from the statue, from Michelangelo."

Philip nodded and walked all the way around the statue. David's buttocks were perfectly carved, and Philip was surprised by his attraction to this part of the anatomy until he remembered how overcome he had been by John's derriere in his tight-fitting fatigues the first time he had seen him in the canteen. When they left the museum, the spell of *David* was broken, and money worries overtook Philip once again.

At dinner, Philip voiced his concern that the remaining money might not last until they got to Venice. John said nothing, and they ate a delicious meal in silence. Walking back to the pensione, John attempted to make light conversation, but this time Philip remained silent.

In the room, John took Philip's hand and led him to the bed. Philip could not resist John's touch. He kissed John with all his strength. He wanted to pour his being into John. They undressed each other, and Philip sank into the bed, with John lying on top of him. Every inch of John's body matched Philip's. He rubbed his penis against Philip's until Philip spread his legs so that John could insert his penis under Philip's testicles, into that space between them and his rectum. John loved to thrust into him as Philip clenched his legs around John's penis. Soon Philip exploded and spewed sperm between them. John came in a puddle on the bed. He liked to tease Philip about how neat his puddle of sperm was compared to Philip shooting all over them.

"There's a hundred babies in that puddle of sperm," joked John.

"Do you want to have one?"

"What?"

"A baby."

"Oh, I don't know," answered John as they drifted off to sleep.

Philip had a fitful sleep and awoke at six. He reached over for John, and his heart sank. He wasn't there. Philip jumped up and ran to the bathroom, despite knowing John would not be there. He stumbled into the desk and saw an envelope. It contained all of John's money and a note he had written: "I realize the worry I've caused you buying the shoes. Here is all the money. I want you to have a good time in Venice. I have my train ticket and am going back to the base. Please have a good time. Love, John."

Philip dressed as fast as he could and ran to the front desk. Luckily, the old woman was already there.

"Mi amigo. Mi amigo. Dove?" he said frantically.

She replied, "Stazione. Lui è partito."

Gone. To the train station. Philip got directions from the woman and ran to the station. He headed for the information booth and discovered that the train for Stuttgart was just leaving. He ran to the track and got there just as the train was pulling out. He ran alongside the train, screaming, "John! John!"

As usual, people were hanging out the windows. They stared at the crazy American and asked each other, "Who is John?" No one knew.

The train left. Tears poured down Philip's face as he turned to go back into the station. And there stood a forlorn John, holding his suitcase. Philip ran to him and kissed him on the lips.

"I missed the train," confessed John.

"Thank God. I would have died without you. Let's get out of Florence and go to Venice."

"Yes, I'm ready to go there."

They raced to the pensione where Philip threw his clothes into his suitcase while John paid the bill. They welcomed the hard seats on the train and settled in, regretting the dark cloud over their last evening in Florence but hoping for a more fulfilling time in Venice. Philip wondered if this was part of getting to know each other, part of developing a relationship, or the pangs of love, and concluded that it was probably all those things. He couldn't stand his jealousy over John. How could he become more secure in John's love for him? How could he believe that John was not going to leave him whenever they had a disagreement?

Venice's romantic atmosphere would conquer any of his doubts—Philip felt certain of it as the train approached the city. As Thomas Mann had written in *Death in Venice*, the city arose out of the mist and sea and was always more impressive than one could imagine. When they arrived at the station, instead of the pavement or street they had expected, they saw a shimmering expanse of water. Buildings were reflected in the canals, bouncing red and blue and golden flashes off the crowd of people. The bombardment of colors fit right in with all the chaos and shouting in foreign languages. They were grateful when an old man grabbed their suitcases and motioned for them to follow him.

The man led them down a narrow street away from the commotion. There it was—a pensione they could afford. The Italians all knew they were American military with little money for a hotel. The smell of sweet tomatoes and garlic wafted out of the boardinghouse. They met the padrone, who told them to come back for dinner. They agreed.

A gondola was parked at the end of the street. A young man around twenty-five, with wavy black hair, smiled and waved them over. "You like ride in gondola?" he managed in English.

"How much?" Philip asked.

"Fifty thousand lire," he replied nonchalantly.

"Tropo," spouted Philip.

"Mama mia. Quanto?" pleaded the gondolier.

"Americano cigarette?" offered Philip.

"Si. Si. Mi piace," the gondolier replied gleefully.

Philip pulled one carton out of his knapsack.

The Italian grabbed it and hid it in his boat. He could sell the cigarettes on the black market. "Veni, veni," he beckoned.

When Philip and John were seated in the gondola, the man threw a blanket to them and winked. Blankets were usually used as lap covers for chilly nights. Although it was a pleasant evening, Philip spread the blanket over their legs so they could hold hands under it.

The gondolier sang as he rowed into the Grand Canal. Other boats floated by, covered with colored lights. As dusk fell, Philip and John moved closer to each other. They didn't know how affectionate they could be, until the gondolier rowed down a dark canal. He turned away from them, supposedly to guide the boat through the passageway, so John took the opportunity to kiss Philip. They pulled the blanket up to their chins so they could embrace and rub into each other. This was the ultimate romantic experience—to be in a gondola in Venice in each other's arms.

The next day, they walked into the bright sunlight on the Rialto Bridge. They were whisked along with a crowd going nowhere. A head bobbed up from the crowd, a blond curly head. A tall blue-eyed cherub smiled at Philip, who was overcome with lust. Although he loved John, he was always susceptible to a muscular blond Adonis.

The god spoke. "Americano?"

John was not fazed. Philip nodded. "Si."

"Io sono Gino."

"I'm Philip, and this is John."

"You have American cigarette?"

"Yes. You like?"

"Si. I work in hotel in Lido. Pay *molto* lire for cigarette."

"How much?"

"You see Lido?"

"No."

"You come to Lido tomorrow. I show you hotel, my room. I get money for cigarette from rich Italian."

"Okay. What time?"

"*Mezzagiorno*. Noon. Excelsior Hotel."

John wondered why Philip was so anxious to go. "Do you like him?" he asked once the interaction was over.

"He's sexy. Would you have a ménage à trois with him?"

"If you want to. I really don't care to, but I'll do it if you want it."

"He's so handsome and sexy. Northern Italians have always attracted me since my family is from the south. The northerners are aloof and feel superior to the southerners. They say, 'Africa begins at Rome.' Maybe I want to pull them down off their high horse by dominating them sexually."

That night they went to Piazza San Marco to visit the cathedral and to see the famed pigeons. They felt as if the statues of the Four Greek Horses on the central balcony would gallop over them; the Carrara marble had a physical power that sent a tingling sensation through their bodies.

John, the artist, explained to Philip the intricacies of the mosaics and the tapestries inside the church. Although John had given up his Catholic religion, he still appreciated the art and music. Philip continued to believe in the Catholic religion, and the appeal of these artistic elements was the only way Philip could get John to go to church.

After the solemnity of the cathedral, they frolicked in the piazza with the pigeons. A vendor sold them birdseed to attract the pigeons. And did it ever attract them, and did they ever attack Philip while John took pictures! They landed on his head, shoulders, arms, and—when he squatted—even his legs. A crowd of onlookers reveled in this phenomenon. Philip begged John to rescue him, and John lovingly complied.

"The birds have made me horny!" exclaimed John.

"Not until we've had a drink in a café," responded Philip.

Cafés all around the piazza had set up tables and chairs of various colors, and each café had its own musicians who filled the air with romantic music. Philip never tired of sitting in an outdoor café and watching people pass by. John, on the other hand, enjoyed looking at Philip and planning a portrait he would make as the changing light shone on Philip's face.

"What are you looking at?" demanded Philip.

"How handsome you are!"

"No one has ever used that adjective to describe me. Intelligent, yes. But handsome, no. Yet you do make me feel beautiful. But you are the beautiful one. I can't compare to you."

"Let's go back to the room. I can't wait another minute."

In the security of their room, where the world could not harm them, they each felt a new freedom with the other's body. Each knew he could do whatever he desired to the other, and the recipient also would love it. Philip loved the back of John's neck. He touched it and kissed it and lovingly bit it. John loved to suck on Philip's nipples until Philip could no longer endure the pleasure and had to have John give him a climax. John gladly took him into his mouth until he exploded.

The Lido promised adventure. Philip and John boarded a vaporetto, a boat for public transportation, which plunged into the lagoon. The waves and the breeze filled them with an intensity to match the blazing sun. Standing at the front of the boat, they could see the Lido emerging from the sea like a narrow long serpent.

John loved the sight but didn't understand why they were going to the Lido to meet a stranger. He wanted to please Philip, so he was willing to participate in whatever activity he desired.

Philip was thrilled at the prospect of having sex with this beautiful stranger. He marveled at the beauty of a person who lived on a small speck of earth on this planet and didn't realize that he could conquer the high life of New York, Paris, or London. He might become an international model or actor but instead was content to live in a small part of the world. By having sex with this muscular, perfect body and seeing him writhe in orgasm, Philip would be sharing in his splendor.

They followed the instructions Gino had given them and walked along the Lungomare Marconi to the Excelsior Hotel, a massive Moorish and Venetian structure. They sat on a bench facing it and waited until the appointed time to meet with Gino. Soon he approached, wearing a white uniform with a gold braid and flashing a captivating smile. His white pants were so tight that every line of his genitalia showed. One could calculate his price per inch for sexual pleasure. In his paltry English he told them that his boss was angry and he could not take them into the hotel, but he had the money for the cigarettes.

Philip immediately realized that all Gino wanted was to make money. He felt deceived by Gino's flirtatious invitation to his room. He knew that jobs were scarce and Gino was trying to make money any way he could.

Philip produced the cigarettes and sadly accepted the money. Gino disappeared into the hotel.

"I'm sorry I put you through this," Philip lamented to John.

"It doesn't matter. We had a beautiful ride over, and now we know what the reality is," offered John.

"You're so wise not to be misled by fantasy. I am learning to appreciate reality from you. Sometimes I forget how lucky I am to have you. Having sex with Gino couldn't compare to making love with you. I do know the difference," confessed Philip.

"It's not a total waste. We had a wonderful ride over. Now let's find a trattoria and have lunch," laughed John.

TEN

Why Did He Do It?

Philip and John carried the sunshine of Italy in their beings when they returned to the base. They were refreshed and ready to work. Even mundane activities were performed without complaint. They approached their work with a renewed vigor that did not go unnoticed, and their captains gave them many compliments. But since passes were hard to come by, they would have to wait for their reward. Confined to the post, they went to the movies, played pool, read, and played records.

However, Philip still worried about the emerald he had dropped when he and Philomena had gone Christmas shopping in Stuttgart. Now it was the day before Christmas, and he was filled with anxiety that he might have to pay for the emerald, despite John's offer to share the burden.

But John proceeded to bring Christmas to their room on the post, in order to share it with their friends Sheldon and Jeremiah. He bought a little Christmas tree that would fit in the corner near the window, and they decorated it within an inch of its life.

The same afternoon they decorated the tree, a soldier came and told Philip to go to the commander's office for a long-distance phone call. Philip ran to the phone since it was an unusual occurrence for a private to receive a telephone call. With trepidation and shaking hands, he grabbed the phone.

A gentle voice with a slight accent said, "I'm sorry to keep you in suspense so long, but we had to send the emerald to the factory." It was the manager of the jewelry store!

"Thank you so much for calling me. What happened with the emerald?"

"They said the stone was not damaged, and they could shave it to smooth it out," the manager said.

"That is the best Christmas present I could have. Is there anything I can do for you?"

"You Americans have done so much for our country that I hope this is a small return."

"It is a huge return for me!"

Philip ran through the quad to a corner where John was working, to tell him they wouldn't have to pay anything on the emerald. John kissed him on the lips.

It was a joy to share the Christmas Eve Midnight Mass in the cathedral in Schwäbisch Gmünd with George and Philomena. Although Philip's feet and legs felt as if they had turned to ice as the cold crept up them from the freezing stone floor, he was happy to be able to sing "Stille Nacht, Heilige Nacht" in its original language. He felt the Baby Jesus in the crèche blessing him and John.

They finished the evening at a gasthaus, where they drank glühwein, a mulled wine that was a German Christmas specialty and that warmed them from the inside out.

Philip and John spent Christmas Day in their room on the

base with Sheldon and Jeremiah. It didn't matter that their friends were not Catholic; the joy of the season was for all. John was enamored with the Roman soldier cameo ring that Philip had bought for him. Philip loved the carved brass jewelry box that John gave him but was disappointed that John had not given him a ring to seal their friendship. John sensed this, and the next day he took his own design of Philip's initials to a jeweler and picked out a 14-karat gold ring for the jeweler to engrave the initials on.

As a reward for their outstanding performance on their jobs, they both had received an overnight pass for after Christmas. They planned to go to Stuttgart to attend a concert and stay overnight, making love in a hotel.

The day of their trip, John said, "I can't go."

Philip was taken aback. "What do you mean?"

"I just can't do it," replied John.

"I don't understand."

"I don't want to have sex," explained John.

"Did something happen?"

"No. I can't do it anymore."

"You don't enjoy it?"

"That isn't it. We are not like that. You know what people say about men who have sex with men."

"Because of the church?"

"I don't give a damn about the church. I left it when I was sixteen."

"Then what is it?"

"I can't explain it."

"Is it because of society? Is it your family?"

"No. That's not who we are. We're not like them."

"We don't have to be like them. We don't have to be like anybody. We're just ourselves. Don't you love me anymore?"

"Of course, I still love you. But I don't want that."

"Please, I don't understand. Don't you want to make love to me?"

"I love you, but not in that way."

"We can still go to Stuttgart. I promise I won't touch you."

"No. I know what will happen. It's not right."

"Don't do this. We don't know when we'll get another pass. You're breaking my heart."

"I'm sorry. I can't do it."

Philip staggered off the post. He took the path through the forest down the mountain to the town. He wandered the streets until he found himself in front of Café Margrit. He went in and had Apfelstrudel mit schlag. He sat dumbfounded. He couldn't think straight. It wasn't possible. What had happened to John? He couldn't bear to speak to anyone, not even a taxi driver, so he walked back up the mountain to the post. He got into bed without saying a word to John. He wanted to sleep forever.

The next day he was greeted by a furious Major Trenton, who said, "There is going to be a court-martial for Jim O'Malley."

"Jim? He's the perfect soldier! What has he done?" Philip thought that if all the rules had been lost, all one had to do was observe Jim. He embodied everything that a soldier stood for.

Not only was he the perfect soldier, but he also could have been the poster boy to entice not-so-handsome men into believing that they might look like him if they would only enlist in the army. Norman Rockwell could not have improved on his all-American-boy look: naturally curly blond hair framing his circular face, circular bright blue eyes, and circular red cheeks. To top it off, he always seemed to be smiling.

Philip could not grasp the concept of being constantly happy in this hellhole army base on top of a mountain in Germany. He remembered the first time he had seen Jim. It had been at a fair in Gmünd. Jim was on a ride that spun in a circle, with centrifugal force holding him up against the wall. His imposing physique dwarfed everyone around him, but it was his big blue eyes and rosy red cheeks that caught Philip's attention. His genuine smile reflected his true enjoyment of this moment of whirling through space.

Jim would often visit Philip and John in their room and speak about his mother, who had recently died. Though normally empathetic, Philip could not bear to listen to the story one more time. He would go off to the poolroom and play by himself while Jim related his story to John, who always listened, and then John would go to the poolroom to get Philip when Jim left their room.

Now this perfect soldier had gone AWOL. The contradiction struck everyone on the base. Why had Jim done it? When the time for the court-martial came, even that process could not wrest the reason from him. All he would say was that he had had to get away.

Philip had been concerned in advance that Jim's court-martial would result in an automatic guilty verdict. The fury and rage of the officers at their favorite creation— Jim, the perfect soldier—was reflected in their decision to punish him to the max. In the drab, gray deliberation room, they asked Philip what could be the reason for Jim's uncharacteristic behavior. Having a bachelor's degree in psychology, Philip donned his psychological hat and stated, "I think he just caved. The pressure and stress of living up to his reputation as the 'perfect soldier' caused him to snap. He couldn't take it anymore, so he did the most opposite thing. He went AWOL and deserted all his military principles." This sounded convincing to the panel of officers—Jim's judges—and convinced them to wait for the decision from the adjunct general in Stuttgart.

Philip, in writing up the report, managed to slip in the exact words of the commanding officer, Colonel Strickland, who had said, "Going AWOL is the worst offense a soldier can commit. True, this is peacetime, but in wartime he could be shot for deserting the army. Going AWOL is worse than rape or murder."

The adjunct general flipped out at the court-martial report, even though he believed the same thing. But civilians might not understand this conviction, and he could not allow the army belief that AWOL was worse than rape or murder to become public knowledge. So he suggested that Jim be given KP as his punishment and that they should extract from him a promise never to commit such a heinous crime again.

After receiving his sentence Jim knew he had Philip to thank for his reprieve. He went to Philip's room and said, "I'd like to thank you somehow. What can I do for you?"

"Nothing. It was nothing. I just hate to see them behave like assholes."

"At least let me buy you some beers tonight."

Since Jim could not leave the post, Philip knew this would have to happen at the beer hall, a prospect he did not relish. The place was cold and damp and packed with smelly soldiers—not his idea of fun. Against his better judgment, he agreed to meet Jim there at 2000 hours.

Contrary to Philip's feelings about Jim, John liked him

and was sympathetic about his mother's death at such an early age. He had even reprimanded Philip once after he had escaped to the poolroom during Jim's visit: "How could you be so cruel to Jim?"

"I feel sorry for him, but I can't listen to him for hours. It is depressing enough to be in the army without adding to it. There's nothing we can do about it."

"You could at least give him some sympathy by letting him talk to get it out."

Philip had said, "I'm sorry. I'm not as patient as you. Why do you have this unusual bond with him? He's nothing like us."

"He is like the boys I grew up with. You are the one who is so different. My background is very different from yours."

"Sure, you were rich. I didn't have a rich daddy to pay for everything. I had to work from the time I was twelve, delivering newspapers."

"I didn't mean different in that way," John said. "I mean you are more cultured and refined. That is what I love about you."

"But not the same way you love Jim."

"I don't love him; I like him as a friend. Listen, why don't you go alone with him sometime and have some beers, so you can get to know him better?"

Now, after the court-martial, seemed to be the time to do it, so Philip did go alone to meet Jim. Once he was there, it seemed incredulous to him that he was sitting opposite Jim in this hellhole to get drunk on five-cent beers.

Surprisingly, after a few minutes, Philip began to take an interest in Jim's recounting of his background. He was not from a rich family at all but had grown up on the South Side of Chicago. Philip was struck by Jim's determination not to end up as a criminal in jail, but to have some dignity in his life. He hadn't waited to be drafted, as Philip had, but had joined the army as a path to a better future. He planned to go to college on the GI Bill and become a teacher. He loved sports and kids, and being a high school coach would fulfill his dreams.

Sensing Philip's interest in what he was saying, Jim pressed his legs on either side of Philip's legs, under the table and out of sight of the others, and remarked, "It's so cold in here. Are you sure you're all right? I wouldn't want you to get sick."

Philip thought this was an explanation for the warmth of Jim's legs squeezing his. It felt like a sensuous cocoon, shielding Philip from the dank surroundings. It also caused him to get an erection. Was this Jim's intent? Straight-arrow Jim making contact with gay Philip—what did it mean?

Perplexed, Philip headed back to the barracks with Jim. Wordlessly, Jim followed Philip to his room. When they got there, they found John passed out on his bunk.

Philip said, "He got a pass and went into town with his drinking buddies. He can't control himself when he's with them."

Philip turned off the light so as not to awaken John. The full moon shone through the thin red gauzelike curtains, giving the room a rosy glow. There were no chairs, so the only place to sit was on Philip's bunk. He and Jim plopped down on it.

"John?" Philip said. "Are you awake?" There was no reply. Philip said to Jim, "I guess he had too much to drink. When he's out with those guys, that's his one weakness. He never goes to the prostitutes or does any of the other stupid things they do."

Feeling a little tipsy themselves, Philip and Jim leaned back against the wall, and the bunk seemed almost like a comfortable sofa. Jim leaned in and kissed Philip on his lips. It seemed so natural that Philip grabbed him and kissed him harder.

"John," whispered Philip, to see if he was really sleeping. He halfway hoped John would wake up and stop them. He didn't. Philip thought about John's rejection of him. He thought John's guilt might stem from an ingrained societal belief that men didn't do such things; men didn't fall in love with other men. It was abnormal. Rarely, John was able to let go of society's reins and allow his true nature to gallop freely in the pleasurable wind of passion. But to Philip it seemed not only natural but also thrilling.

Although Philip was not entirely convinced that John had passed out, he could not resist when Jim pulled him down on the bunk. Jim placed his head on Philip's crotch and ground his own crotch into Philip's face.

Philip asked, "Have you ever done it with a guy?" He was hoping for the right answer, since now he knew he had to go all the way with him.

"Once, with a buddy when we went to Florida on spring break. There was only one bed, and we'd had a lot to drink. We sucked each other off, and it was great. That was the only time I did it. But I want to do it with you."

"Are you sure it's not just because I helped you?"

"Hell no. I'm really attracted to you. I don't know how it happened, but I want to make love to you."

Jim tore open Philip's pants and pulled out his hard cock. He devoured it. Philip gasped and did the same thing to Jim. They didn't dare take off their clothes, since the sergeant could come in for bed check at any time. However, their passion pushed them over the edge, and they simultaneously came into each other's mouth. Usually, Philip didn't like to swallow, but Jim's cum tasted like peppermint. They quickly buttoned their pants and jumped up from the bunk.

Jim implored, "I have to see you again, like this."

Philip responded, "You know that I'm with John."

"Yes, but I don't care. Whenever you can do it again, please tell me."

"I'll try."

Philip was in a quandary about what he would do now, with both Jim and John.

ELEVEN

Trying to Live in the Moment

The next day, out of the blue, John said, "Let's go to our room in town."

"Do you really want to?" asked Philip, confused since John had recently shattered their plans to go to Stuttgart, saying he couldn't do this anymore.

"Yes, I really want to go."

"That's the only thing I want to do," replied Philip.

"I know how much it hurt you when I said I wouldn't go to Stuttgart. Sometimes I let the world interfere. I'm sorry."

They didn't want to wait for a taxi, so they ran down the path to the town. They enjoyed walking through the Marktplatz. After that it wasn't far to their house. As soon as they entered their room, they clung to each other. They would request another leave as soon as possible to escape the atmosphere of the army. They needed a beautiful environment in which their love could flourish.

The leave they hoped for was granted, for August.

In the meantime, once again they had to go on maneuvers

in the field. They were ready to endure any tortures, as long as they knew they could get away on leave afterward.

Whenever it was time to go to the field, the army had a unique gift for finding unexplored forests in Bavaria. This time was no exception. The vegetation was dense, and the soldiers had to clear out places to erect their tents. They were constantly supervised or given duties to keep them busy, with their only breaks occurring at mealtime.

"I have to be alone with you for a few minutes, or I'll go crazy," Philip told John at lunch one day.

"Let's cut our meal short tonight at supper and take a walk in the woods," John suggested.

They held hands for the first time in days as they strolled through the fading light streaming through the tall *Tulpenbaum* trees, looking for a more private place. As soon as Philip spotted it, he knew it would be ideal—a trench carved in the earth, about eight feet long and four feet deep. He jumped into it and coaxed John to join him. He lay in the dirt, and John lay on top of him. They kissed and rubbed against each other, leaving behind the grime of army life.

They vaguely became aware of a snorting sound. John, who was more alert, said, "It's getting louder."

Philip said, "I can't imagine what it could be."

"I overheard the captain talking about wild boars in these woods. Do you think it could be that?"

"I don't even know what a wild boar is."

"I know they can attack you and gore you, like a bull."

The pounding of hooves and the snorting grew louder. The two defenseless soldiers remained in their horizontal position, all passion drained from them. They didn't dare look up but felt certain it was a wild boar up there, near the trench. They whispered soothing words to each other as the boar thundered around above them. After what seemed like an eternity, they were relieved to hear the sound of hooves moving away from them. They scrambled up from the ditch and silently made their way back to camp.

The next morning, Philip hurriedly got dressed and went to John's barracks. John had been given permission to use the makeshift showers. Although Philip was fully clothed, he entered the anteroom to the showers. John was drying himself, so Philip sat on a bench to wait for him. The room was filled with steam and heat, but Philip was determined to wait it out.

John remarked, "I have a crick in my neck."

Dale, a rugged southerner just out of the shower, approached him. "I can give you a rubdown."

John replied, "Thanks, but it's just my neck and shoulders."

Dale, in all his nudity, stood behind John, who was still naked, and began to massage his neck and shoulders. Dale's huge penis was beginning to lengthen into a semierection, a fraction of an inch away from John's ass. Philip tried to be nonchalant as he kept his focus on Dale's penis to be sure it did not touch John, who continued to carry on a normal conversation, in spite of a number of suggestive remarks made by Dale.

When John had dried and dressed, he and Philip left the showers. John seemed perplexed over Philip's silence. "What's the matter?"

Philip responded, "Did you like his big prick?"

"What do you mean?"

"It was practically touching your ass."

"I didn't feel his dick."

"He wanted to shove it in your ass."

"Nothing happened. Why are you so jealous?"

"Because of the suggestive remarks he made to you."

"I have to work with him. You know that all those guys talk like that. He's been making comments about you and me being lovers. It doesn't help when you have to sit in the showers and watch me as if I were a child."

"I'm sorry. I know I get crazy whenever anyone is attracted to you."

"You know I would never do anything with another man. You are the only one. I don't even think of men in that way."

"It's hard to believe that you could have sex with me and not even be attracted to another handsome, sexy male."

"It's true. You are the only one." John had to get to work. "Will you meet me at lunchtime in that grove of flowering trees?"

Philip had a sudden feeling of dread, but he answered, "Okay."

When they met, John said, "We have to stop this. We can't go on. Someone is going to find out."

Philip looked up at the pink and white feathery flowers on the trees, framed by the bright blue sky, and said, "Okay, we won't see each other until we get back to the post."

John insisted, "I mean we won't see each other anymore."

Philip felt his head cave into his neck, the two of which proceeded to fall into his chest and stomach, where his internal organs collapsed into his legs and feet, and he fell to the ground. "Please don't do this," he begged as he continued to look up at the flowering trees. *If those delicate, wispy flowers can survive, so can I.* Later, he would feel that it was important for him to learn the name of this area—Naturschutzgebiet Rinntal bei Alfeld—where a momentous event in his life had occurred. "I won't come near you while we're in the field. Can we talk about this when we get back to the post?"

John eased his harsh stance. "Okay, I'll wait until we get back."

Zombielike, Philip continued his office work. He was glad there were no courts-martial, only mundane paperwork. He felt ripped open by John. Did this mean that John didn't love him anymore? Had he fallen in love with another soldier?

These thoughts made Philip gravitate toward Lieutenant Diekert. He was of German descent but had been born in Connecticut and had attended West Point. He was planning to go to Princeton when he got discharged. He already had the clean-cut preppy look and a serious expression on his face. He was most efficient and always requested Philip to type his documents. He was not much older than Philip, and they soon developed an easy rapport with each other.

After an afternoon of intensive work, Lieutenant Diekert offered to drive Philip to his field barracks in his jeep.

When they arrived, Philip knew that John would be waiting for him for dinner; they were still bunk mates and had to do some things together. Philip jumped out of the jeep and shouted, "Thanks for the ride, Lieutenant!" He knew John could hear him. He wanted John to know that he could get this handsome lieutenant if he wanted.

They ate dinner in silence and got into their bunks to read, Philip on the top bunk and John on the bottom one. Philip was preoccupied with listening for John's every movement and wondered if John was doing the same for him. Eventually, they fell asleep.

A crash and the sound of grinding metal woke them up. Dale—the soldier Philip had seen in the locker room with John—was drunk and was screaming, "You fucking Jew!" Dale had punched Sheldon and knocked him into the wood-burning stove, which was lit. Everyone woke up to sparks flying out of the stove.

There were eight or ten soldiers billeted there, and they all saw Sheldon being beaten, but no one said a word. Each man had his own reason for not getting involved. Philip was afraid that Dale would turn his rage on him and say something about his relationship with John. John was afraid that Dale would reveal that he knew the truth about him and Philip. Lucas, the strong black soldier who had tormented David Smith, didn't want to risk having Dale call him derogatory names. And so it went, with no one going to Sheldon's aid as Dale continued to punch him mercilessly.

Sheldon didn't make a sound.

Dale's blows sounded like thunder. He knocked Sheldon into the metal stove again, screaming, "You kike! It's your people that are ruining the world. You think that you are so fucking smart. If you're so smart, why don't you fight back? The Nazis should've put you in the gas chamber here!" He caught his breath for the next blow and then spat out, "You bastard Jew! If you didn't own all the banks, my father would have gotten a loan for the farm. You deserve to suffer, you greedy Jew!"

Philip prayed that the drunken Dale would stop or that someone would stop him. But no one did. He could hear John breathing heavily in the bunk below him and knew that he was wondering if they should stop Dale. It was a nightmare with no end. Where was the sergeant for bed check?

Sheldon took blow after blow without uttering a word, just an occasional gasp from the pain. Blow after blow knocked him into the stove or the wall, until finally, he fell to the floor.

Suddenly, there was silence. Then Dale and Sheldon retreated to their respective bunks. The next day, Philip and

John didn't know what to say to Sheldon; they both felt ashamed over not having helped him. Sheldon mustered all his courage and didn't tell anyone what had happened to him. They respected his decision and never said a word about it. However, their friendship had been permanently altered.

✛

When maneuvers in the field were over and Philip and John returned to the army base, they sat in their room, staring at each other. They were shaken by the events that had taken place on the field trip. They were uncertain about their upcoming leave to go to Spain. Most important, they were uncertain about their relationship in the future.

Soon it was time for them to go to Barcelona. They took a train to Cannes, where they would stay overnight. Once they had found a reasonably priced hotel, they wandered the streets of the city. Philip was interested in seeing the site of the Cannes Film Festival, whereas John was interested in the natural beauty of the coast.

On one of the dark twisting streets, they encountered a convertible car. Two beautiful French women called out to them. When they walked over to the car, they discovered that the women were prostitutes. The girls told them that they were so cute that they would take both of them for the price of one.

Philip asked John, "Do you want to go with them?"

"No!"

Philip was not sure how to interpret this. Did it mean that John still cared for him or that John was just not interested in a prostitute? He wondered what would happen when they reached Barcelona.

TWELVE

The Other Side of Paradise

On the train heading for Barcelona, they talked about how exciting it would be to see a bullfight and discussed passages from Hemingway's *The Sun Also Rises*. Although they did not relish the killing of a bull, they did want to see all the pageantry and beauty that accompanied the corrida.

As the train went along the coast of France, Philip and John had an ingenious idea—to search the train for more comfortable seating. They found an empty first-class compartment, where each one would have an entire long plush velvet seat to lie down on. They closed the door and pulled down the drapes, so no one could look in.

However, after about an hour, an inquisitive porter opened the door and saw them lying on the seats. He asked for their first-class tickets, which they did not have, and then demanded their passports. They had to give him their US Army IDs, which served as their passports. He snatched their ID cards and ran out the door and down the corridor, screaming, "I'll turn you in at the next stop!"

They ran after him, with Philip pleading, "Please, we have to have our army IDs. That is something that we cannot lose."

The porter continued to run and to berate them. "You have no right to be in first class when you did not pay for it."

Philip and John were shaking with anxiety as the porter continued to scream. Suddenly, the man stopped and pointed to the window. They looked out and saw the Mediterranean Sea, and the porter exclaimed, "La mer!"

The three of them stood in silence for about a minute, admiring the beautiful sea. Then the porter again took up his screaming and running, and they were all off on their chase down the corridor. Philip and John caught up with the man and paid him off to get their army IDs back. He was happy to accept their money and return their IDs.

A kaleidoscope of colors and sweet smells greeted the train as it pulled into the station. The gentleman in the information booth was most helpful, considering that he had little grasp of English. He understood that they were American soldiers and didn't have much money. He wrote the name of a boardinghouse on a piece of paper and assured them it was clean and cheap.

When they arrived at the house, a pleasant, plump housewife greeted them and led the way to a room. The whole place had a family atmosphere, and they were immediately convinced to accept it.

They had not touched each other since they had gone on maneuvers in the field, but during the hours on the train from Cannes, passion had been building in each of them. As soon as the woman left and the door closed behind her, John took Philip's hand, in a gesture signaling his wish to make up, and led him to the bed. They fell on the bed and kissed. Their longing exploded as they pulled each other's clothes off.

Their nude bodies melded into each other, and the heat of the summer day only contributed to the passion emanating from their bodies. They slipped into the hollow at the center of the bed as Philip mounted John, awakening each nerve and cell as they pressed into each other. Their penises hardened as only young men's could.

Philip's penis found its home alongside John's penis. He thrust up and down with all his might. John's legs gripped Philip's torso, and he rose to meet each thrust. In seconds they were spewing their cum all over each other. John's lips were swollen from the pressure of Philip's mouth as Philip tried to crawl inside him. They continued to lie in their sweat because the afterglow was so comforting. Nothing else in the world mattered. They had earned this moment of peace and heart-piercing love.

A huge chifforobe standing on one wall of their room and prints of bullfighters on the other gave them the feeling that the room was a safe cave for them. Even the windows did not intrude upon their safety from the rest of the world. In fact, Philip and John delighted in looking out at the courtyard below, where strings of laundry blew in the breeze. Philip didn't know why, but he knew that this image would imprint upon his brain and remain with him for the rest of his life.

Following directions given by the owner of the boarding-house, Philip and John left for their first adventure in the city: climbing the rickety wooden stairs of an ancient building to reach the gnarled old women who stitched colored gems into the flamboyant, intricate patterns that decorated the jackets of the matadors, each gem sewn by hand. The women could sense the appreciation of the two Americans, and without speaking a word of English, they communicated surprise and joy at the visit. However, the women could not lower the price of the shimmering jackets enough that the soldiers could afford to buy them. Even a bright pink matador's cape was too costly. John urged Philip to buy one of the gem-encrusted jackets anyway, but Philip knew that would not leave enough money for the rest of the trip. Philip was not terribly disappointed that they could not buy such a treasure, because they carried the aura of its beauty with them when they left.

The day of the bullfight filled them with wonder. When they reached the arena, the waves of excitement that washed over them from the crowd were as vibrant as the rays of the sun. Their bodies vibrated from the sound made by hordes of people yelling and screaming the names of the matadors. The closest thing to this kind of pandemonium that either Philip or John had ever experienced was at a rock concert—and in fact, the bullfighters were the rock stars of Spain.

They bought seats close to the ring so that they would experience everything. Horns blared as the bull was released into the ring. Then came the banderilleros, who teased the bull and stabbed colorful poles into his neck and back. Philip thought it was somewhat cruel, since the bull hadn't done anything to provoke that. Then picadors on horseback stuck the bull with lances, causing deep wounds and sending blood flowing, while they attempted to tire the bull. The bull retaliated by goring the horses, which were blindfolded and wore thick padding. This was very upsetting to John, who had ridden horses when he was growing up in California. Philip cringed at the sight of blood pouring from the bull.

When the matador entered, he was as graceful as a ballet dancer. The visual aspect of this appealed to John, whereas Philip was caught up in the ritual. The matador made sweeping passes and defied the bull to gore him. Finally, the matador buried his sword between the shoulder blades of the bull. With the sword still in him, the bull staggered a few steps toward the edge of the ring where Philip and John sat. Philip rose and stared directly into the eyes of the bull. The bull stared back, and then his knees buckled, and he died, still looking at Philip, who was shaking. Philip felt the power of the death of the bull, but he didn't understand his own reaction. He felt that somehow this was something he was not supposed to have seen.

John grabbed Philip and led him out of the stadium.

After the bullfight, both Philip and John needed a pleasant change of scenery. They learned about a romantic boat ride from Barcelona to Majorca. With John speaking his California Spanish, they found a travel agent, who booked them a sleeper on the boat.

At midnight a taxi took them to the dock. Everything seemed mysterious and wonderful. They had a room just a little larger than the double bed in it. That was all they needed. They gently removed their clothing, which they would have to wear when disembarking the ship. Philip luxuriated in lying on the fluffy bed. John crawled on top of him and kissed his eyelids. "I love the smell and texture of your skin," John said as he kissed Philip's nose and ears and lips.

Philip held on to him as John kissed his way down to Philip's chest. He always gasped at John's lips caressing his nipples. No one else had ever done that to him. He grabbed John's head because of the almost unbearably thrilling sensation. Then John poured his love onto Philip's cock. He kissed it, licked it, and devoured it to its root. Philip sprang up in response to the pleasure soaring through his body. He screamed, "John! Oh, John! I love you. I love your mouth on my cock. I don't ever want you to stop. I'm going to cum." He exploded sweetness and saltiness down John's throat and felt that John was a part of him.

All night they made love and occasionally dozed off. As the sun came up, the boat docked at Palma de Majorca, which rose from the sea in spikes of blue, beige, crimson, and all the colors of the rainbow. Philip and John also rose from their bed, glowing and energized. The island in the sea made them feel that they had lost the rest of the world. They were in a fresh new cocoon. They fearlessly disembarked and headed for the cathedral in Palma de Majorca.

The entrance to the cathedral was breathtaking. Ironically, the foundation for the cathedral, laid in 1230, was on the site of a former mosque, so the building faced Mecca instead of Jerusalem. But the purpose of a Gothic cathedral—to propel one toward a higher power—was fulfilled. The nave was so high that Philip and John were forced to look up toward the light streaming through. Of the ninety stained-glass windows, their favorite was the rose window, the largest round stained-glass window in the world. It featured red cherries with blue and green leaves, with yellow and white flowers surrounding the cherries. John was swept away into the artistry of the Gothic cathedral, while Philip was inclined more toward the spiritual aspect.

After the splendor of the cathedral, they boarded a bus that traveled along the coastline. Each beach they passed was more beautiful than the one before. But finally, there it was just ahead of them—their dream beach—and they asked the bus driver to let them off. With one suitcase each, they stumbled through the sand toward a bronze-colored wooden inn. It was new but looked as if it had held a thousand romances. The lovely proprietress showed them a double room with a private bath. They took it without asking the price. The floor was made of wooden slats with space between them so that sand from the beach could be swept through the space into the earth below. It gave the room the appearance of floating in space.

When the proprietress lingered, talking with them, Philip became agitated and nervous. He bounced from foot to foot as if he had to pee. John, on the other hand, spoke joyfully to the woman. She gave them a tourist brochure that listed the sights of the town and the beaches.

Finally, Philip grabbed John's arm and said, "We have to unpack, or all our clothes will be wrinkled."

"Don't worry," the proprietress said. "I'll iron them for you, no charge." She laughed as she was leaving the room.

Philip pulled John onto the bed and pressed his body, head to toe, against John's. They melted into each other, one human flesh-and-blood statue. They kissed, sending heat throughout their bodies. They pressed harder into each other. Philip hugged the back of John's neck, his favorite nongenital part. He played with the scraggly hair lining John's neck. He loved the rounded flesh of his neck. Immediately, that gave him an erection. He pressed his penis against John's already hard penis.

"I have to have it," Philip gasped.

"I want it just as much. My balls are starting to hurt," moaned John.

Philip began the descent to John's penis. He kissed the front of his neck as he unbuttoned his short-sleeved grayish patterned shirt. He wondered where John had gotten this shirt since he liked it and wore it so often. The cotton was soft and soothing against his cheek as he kissed John's nipples. He blew on them and sucked them until John jumped. He looked into John's eyes and had never seen anyone else look at him that way. John's eyes made him feel beautiful and complete. He felt truly himself, with no fears distorting his being. He did not have to hide anything about himself. He could just be and know that he was entirely accepted by John.

John helped to unbutton his own shirt and began to unbutton Philip's. John's naked chest took Philip's breath away. He snuggled into it as if it were a cove in the coastline of the dangerous world.

After showering, they found their way to the dining room and learned that all meals would be provided. That meant they would never have to leave this spot, and they seldom did.

Was it the sun and sand and ocean? Was it the luscious oranges, lemons, limes, grapes, and pineapples pouring their potent juices into them? Was it the sturdy date palm, the arbutus strawberry tree, and the crunchy figs that strengthened their spirit? Whatever it was, something ignited a passion in them that would last for their entire stay.

Although their routine was the same, it never bored them. In the morning they woke up and had sex before going to the bathroom. They could not wait another waking moment without touching and kissing each other. After the refreshing water of the shower poured over them, they went to breakfast and then to the private beach, where they would dive into the surf and lie on a blanket warmed by the hot sand. They softly spoke and smiled at the other residents on the beach but had no need to engage in conversation with them. Before lunch they returned to their room to shower and race to the bed. Even though they had had sex in the morning, their desire was stronger than ever. Each ravished the other's body, and then they ravished their lunch. Then it was back to the beach to lie with legs touching while they read until the sun sank into the sea. They returned to their room again to shower and eat the most delicious supper ever. Although their hunger was sated, their craving for each other mounted. They immediately undressed and got into bed and comforted their naked bodies. There was no end to their passion.

One night John became more adventurous. He said, "Let's try something."

Naturally, Philip was only too eager. As he watched, John went into the bathroom and shortly returned to their bed. John lay on his stomach and commanded Philip to get on him. As Philip mounted him, he felt John's hand on his penis with something wet and smooth.

"Put it in me," ordered John.

Philip awkwardly placed his penis at the opening of John's rectum and gently inserted his penis. Philip was surprised by how easily it went in. "What did you put on it?"

"Soap," answered John.

Philip thrust in and out until they both screamed with pleasure as Philip came inside John, triggering John's orgasm.

Philip was shocked at having entered another man. The only form of intercourse he had had previously was with Helene, his acting partner in New York. They had been friends for two years, and nothing romantic had happened except onstage. In acting class they had performed a scene from *Ah, Wilderness* in which she had played the prostitute and seduced Eugene, Philip's character. When her seduction really worked, Philip had blushed and stammered. He was upset by the laughter from the audience when they realized what was really happening to him. When he had visited her later, while on leave from the army, apparently his uniform turned her on. With Helene, he felt that it was time to experience a woman, since he was approaching twenty-three years of age. She was older and experienced and was gentle in her guidance of Philip's penis to her vagina. When he was inside her, he had thought, *This is what Julius Caesar felt when he fucked Cleopatra.*

After John sprayed the sheets with his sperm, Philip withdrew, and they ran to the bathroom. Philip vigorously washed his penis as John stuck a washcloth into his rectum.

"I don't recommend using soap," John said. "It burns like hell."

They laughed and agreed to use Vaseline next time. They had just discovered that anal intercourse was very pleasurable.

"Next time you can jerk me off as you fuck me. I love the feel of your hand on my dick," announced John.

Afterward, they dressed in sports coats to go for the first time to a nearby restaurant they had discovered.

Walking along the trail in the dunes and brush, Philip was strangely silent; he himself didn't know why. John was puzzled at his silence too.

"Are you upset because I changed my role?" asked John.

"I'm surprised. I never knew you wanted to do that. I always loved you on top of me. Had you ever done that before?"

"Once, at boarding school. Another boy and I ran up a hill and hid behind a tree. The other boys couldn't see us. He was a fat kid and was gasping for air as he grabbed on to me. His hand slipped down to my dick. 'What are you doing?' I asked. 'I'll let you stick it in me,' the fat boy told me. 'You'll like it. It really feels good.' He unzipped my pants and pulled out my penis, and then he pulled down his own pants. He spit into his hand and rubbed it on my penis and guided it to his rear end. He pushed my penis into his rectum, and I actually saw stars. I instinctively pushed in farther, and the fat boy bucked up against me, and I thrust until I came inside him." John continued, "Tonight I wanted to see what it felt like to have *you* inside me. Is it all right?"

"Yes, I was just surprised. We can do it again, and this time you can come in me. Then we'll be part of each other."

They soon reached the restaurant, which was open to the sky. White walls rose about ten feet into the air, but there was no ceiling, and white umbrellas topped white tables, in sharp contrast to the midnight-blue sky and stars overhead.

John asked, "Are you still upset?"

Philip replied, "I was surprised. Did you like me fucking you? Was I good enough?"

"Oh yes. I loved it. I wanted it to make us closer. I felt your cock inside me and cum through my whole body. Did you like it?"

"I did, but I like it better when you are on top of me."

"We can always do that. I just thought it would be good to try something different. But you know I always cum when I'm humping you. I love the feel of your balls on my cock as I press it into your crotch. Are you okay?"

"Yes. I just need time to think. I do want you inside me. I'm just confused now."

"We don't have to do it again if you don't want to."

"I want to do everything with you."

"We'll work it out."

They enjoyed a Spanish meal and then held hands in the darkness while walking back to their hotel. They couldn't go to sleep until they rubbed each other to orgasm.

The next day, they went to the drugstore and bought Vaseline. They had read in porn stories about guys using Vaseline. Philip lay on his side, and John greased his penis with Vaseline and pushed into Philip's rectum. The sudden invasion into virgin territory caused Philip to scream.

John stopped. "Did I hurt you?"

"No, it's okay," Philip lied. "Keep going."

Eventually, the pain subsided, and a new sensation flooded Philip's anus, so he bucked back against John to derive as much pleasure as possible. At the time, Philip didn't realize that John's penis was larger than average.

After five days of continuous lovemaking and countless orgasms, they clung to each other in bed. John broke the blissful silence. "I know the world will never let us live the way we want. This has been paradise."

Suddenly, the sky dimmed to a slate gray. Rain began to dance on their woven bamboo roof.

"Let's have a suicide pact. We can die in ecstasy," John implored.

The rain slashed against their room, and booms of thunder caused it to shake. Lightning lit up the furious ocean, and they could see it devouring the beach and threatening the inn.

Philip knew that John was deadly serious. It frightened him to think that he had caused John to love him so much that John would die for him.

Philip reasoned, "It's been so wonderful that we've lost touch with reality. We have to go back to our real life in the army and then decide if we want to do that."

The storm abated into a gentle rain that sang along the bamboo covering their room.

John said, "We could live here when we get discharged. It's not very expensive."

"We could. You could paint, but I couldn't act here."

John argued, "You could write. The skit you wrote for the officers' Sadie Hawkins Day was great. You have a talent for writing."

"I wish we could have seen that production, but they

wouldn't let me take you to the Officers' Club, so I didn't go either."

Both were silent for a while. Then Philip said, "I think we should leave a day early. Let's not take a chance of spoiling this wonderful leave. We can get back to the base and have a day to get our gear in order."

As they were leaving their room the next day, another gay couple arrived. One of them gushed, "We are so happy you are leaving today because it gives us a chance to get this room."

Philip smiled. "We have enjoyed it immensely. I hope you have as good a time as we had."

The couple gave them knowing looks and smiles.

THIRTEEN

A Trip to Stuttgart

In an attempt to rejoin the real world after their ex-perience of paradise in Majorca, Philip had planned another trip to Stuttgart to visit Ann and Judy, his college friends from Canada. His married friends George and Philomena had suggested some time ago that they would like to meet the girls too and would be happy to drive him and John in their Volkswagen.

Now they were on the way, accompanied also by Jim and by Damian, a new friend from the army post at the bottom of the mountain. You could pack several people into a Volkswagen bug, if they were on intimate terms. George and Philomena sat in the front seat; in the back seat, Philip, Damian, Jim, and John sat upright, with squeezed arms and legs. This uncomfortable seating arrangement notwithstanding, they were all happy to have a few hours' leave from their dreary post on the mountain in Schwäbisch Gmünd.

As they'd told Philip during their trip to the base, Ann and Judy had managed to secure jobs in the American PX in Stuttgart during their grand tour of Europe. Philip had always thought of Ann as the adventurous one, not worrying about consequences, and Judy as the practical one. He wanted Damian to meet Judy, in hopes that a relationship would develop, even though he knew that Damian was attracted to him. Philip felt a lustful pull toward Damian, but he thought that Damian was too naive about the consequences of having a sexual relationship with a man.

To pass the time while speeding on the autobahn, they sang all the patriotic American songs they knew. They gave thanks, each in their own way, that the army had stationed them in this beautiful Bavarian countryside. Nature was always present in the towns and cities, so life was more humane and genteel than in many American cities. Perhaps that contributed to the blossoming tender feelings that Philip could feel emanating from these mostly heterosexual men. Being king of the campus was not something he had experienced in college, so Philip was floating on a warm sea of contentment.

The men pressed against each other in the car without any tension. The warmth of legs and arms was like a beautiful, soothing cocoon for the four men, and they relished their new sensual experience.

Ann and Judy were excitedly awaiting their arrival. They had even told their German landlords about their expected visitors, so that they would not get the wrong idea. The wife was more liberal than the husband and winked the other way whenever the girls had a male visitor. Now, with four single men coming to visit, she had baked traditional German kuchen to welcome them, hoping a couple of them might develop a relationship with the girls.

The girls and the landlord and his wife all ran out of the house to meet the American visitors. Ann and Judy were filled with excitement, and they ran in a circle around the soldiers as if they were running around a Christmas tree. Seeing friends from home was a rare occurrence in the military environment. It was something one didn't even dream of; the army's strict rules and regulations were in sharp contrast to the familiarity of their past loves and friendships. The excitement was so contagious that the German landlords felt as if they had known the Americans all their lives. Philip tried to take Ann aside to tell her that John was his lover, but he didn't have a chance. Everyone was kissing and hugging them.

The tiny apartment was cozy. The girls had cooked a real meal, which everyone ate while sitting on pillows on the floor and balancing plates on their lap.

John said, "Tell us about your trip to Greece."

Ann said, "It was fantastic. Neither of us had ever been there before. The sea and the sun were different from Toronto."

Judy added, "I actually wore a bikini. For the first time in my life, I did not feel self-conscious about my body. The Greek people are very accepting of all shapes and sizes."

"We got used to running around in shorts and sandals, and when we got to Germany, that was a problem," Ann explained.

"You won't believe this," Philip laughingly told the others. "These two vestal virgins arrive in our little German town, and no one will give them a room. No room at the inn 'for girls like you,' said the proprietor. The way they were dressed, he thought they were prostitutes."

Jim asked, "What did you do? Where did you sleep?"

"The irony," said Ann, "was that the best hotel in Schwäbisch Gmünd—and the most expensive—was the only one that would give us a room."

Judy chimed in, "At least now we were high-class prostitutes!"

It felt good for everyone to enjoy a belly laugh. That didn't happen very often on the post.

Damian suggested, "Would you please put on those clothes from Greece?"

Ann said, "I think I hid them."

But then Judy piped up. "I know where they are. I'll get them."

"No, no!" cried Ann.

"Please," everyone begged, except George's wife Philomena.

Philomena tried to intercede for Ann and said, "Don't embarrass them."

Philip pleaded, "We're your best friends. Please give us some entertainment."

A few minutes later, Judy made her entrance first, her hair flying askew. Her shirt was tied at the waist, exposing her belly button; her shorts were cut off up to her ass; and she was wearing open-toed sandals. Someone put seductive music on the record player, and everyone cheered and hollered as Judy danced around the room.

Then Ann ventured forth in a similar getup, which looked comical on her, but everyone cheered just the same, and Ann screwed up enough courage to dance to the sensuous music too. Again there were cheers, and Philip got up to dance with her.

All the others, fueled by German wine, got up to dance too, with or without a partner. Philip tried to steer Ann into the next room to tell her about his relationship with John, but he was unable to do so with everyone cutting in. So he floated along with the crowd.

Jim grabbed Philip and held him close. He whispered, "I have to see you again. I've been thinking about what we did, and I get so horny I could explode. When can we do it? I don't care where. Right here in the bathroom, now!"

Philip tried to reason with him. "I want to do it, but we have to be sensible. Everyone would see us go in there. You know that I was with John first. That is my relationship."

Jim said, "I won't interfere in your relationship. But this is different. I have to have you. I've never felt like this. Just let me touch your cock."

"No. Everyone can see us. I'm going to stop dancing now, so please don't make a scene," he said, with a question in his voice.

"If you promise we can do it tomorrow," demanded Jim.

"Okay, I promise," Philip spat as he moved away.

Just then Damian staggered over to Philip and said, "Let's dance. I've never danced with a guy." He pulled Philip in so close that Philip could feel Damian's erection. "Why won't you do it with me?" Damian asked. "I know you do it with the other guys. What's wrong with me?"

"Have you ever done it with a guy?" asked Philip.

"No."

"Then why do you want to do it with me? And why now?"

"I just feel I want to be naked with you and touch you."

"It isn't as simple as that. There are consequences. It doesn't stop there. What if you fall in love with me?"

"I already am in love with you."

"You know that John and I are lovers."

"I don't care. I'll do whatever you want. I just want to be near you. No one has ever been so kind to me."

"I like you. You're a nice guy. Don't worry about the other guys in your barracks. They're assholes. You don't need them for friends. Let them call you names. You're more refined than they are. Do you think they have silk wall coverings like you have in your home in Texas?" Philip was struck by the contrast between his rough-and-tumble mental image of Texas and this rich and delicate boy living in such a house.

Judy waltzed over to Damian and coaxed him into dancing with her. George and his wife were dancing, probably for the first time since their wedding. He looked turned on and kissed her with a real force.

Damian and Jim managed to corner Philip and push him out to dance, with one in front and one in back. They both pressed their erections into Philip until he was sweating and breathing heavily. His brain said this would have to stop, especially in front of the girls.

Philip had to get out. Suddenly, he was at the window, which was now open since the temperature of the room had risen considerably with all the body heat. It appeared that he was only on the first floor, so he jumped out of the window. He landed with a crash and felt his legs go into his pelvis. The girls screamed, and the men ran out to get him. Philip was in shock as he rolled on the sidewalk. He was bruised from landing on the pavement, but other than that, no harm had been done, and nothing was broken.

The guys carried Philip back into the house. Worried to death, John asked, "How could you do such a thing? Why?"

"I don't know," Philip answered sincerely, and they all burst into laughter.

They ate more delicious German pastry and prepared to drive back to Schwäbisch Gmünd. Again, George and his wife sat in the front seat; it was their car. However, there were no complaints as the guys piled on top of one another in the back seat. They were mellow and pliable, wrapping arms and legs around each other, with Philip as the focal point.

When George turned the car onto the treacherous

autobahn, John kissed Philip. Damian nibbled on Philip's ears, and Jim felt Philip's cock. They kissed and rubbed him all over. It was heavenly and pleasurable for the first half hour, but then Philip tired of it and tried to stop them. But once in motion, there was no stopping the passion train. It traveled from the top of Philip's head to his toes. Someone removed his shoes and sucked his toes. Never had Philip even dreamed that one man, let alone three, that he was attracted to—and that he thought was among the most handsome and sexy of the thousand soldiers on his post—would actually desire him in return. It was what he had prayed for in college. And now, three years later, it was happening.

Philip was at a loss when he felt their tears and heard their pleas for his love. He was worried about George and Philomena in the front seat, but it seemed that the noise from the autobahn created a protective shell and shut them out. He didn't know what to do about John, who was supposed to be his boyfriend. Philip satisfied the other two by telling them that he would meet with them tomorrow and they would sort it out.

When George dropped them off at the post, each one went to his barracks. Philip looked up to the starlit sky and knew that this was a moment to cherish, a moment that would never happen again.

FOURTEEN

No Regard for Another's Life

It was 1961, and both Philip and John were scheduled to be discharged before the year was over—John in July and Philip in September.

Being in the army in Germany provided them with an incredible benefit—they could be discharged and remain in Germany, if they wished. John did wish. He would have an unemployment check for his two years' service in the army, and it could be forwarded to him in Germany. He and Philip already had a room in Anna's house, for twelve American dollars a week. They could live there until they had saved enough money to move to Majorca. They could have it all. John would say, "We'll be two old men sitting by the fireplace with our dogs and smoking our pipes."

Philip loved that picture, but there was a tiny ember burning from his past: ambition. He had to be famous. Hundreds of years of the poverty of his ancestors in Italy prevented them from rising above their station in life. He had known from early childhood that he did not want the life his parents had. He wanted to live like the glamorous people in the movies, traveling to exotic lands and having romantic affairs with handsome men.

This was not what John wanted. He didn't need to be a famous artist like Picasso. He didn't need everyone in the world to know who he was.

Philip craved adoration for his art; he wanted strangers to acclaim his glory, to prove that his life had a purpose. He couldn't understand why John didn't want the same for himself. He couldn't understand why they couldn't be together and have all that.

Philip tried to be reasonable about the situation. He loved his portrait that John had painted, but he had no way of knowing whether John was a good artist and would become a great one like Picasso. If that was possible, Philip was willing to make sacrifices for John the way Picasso's women had. In fact, they hoped to visit Picasso, who was living in the south of France. Philip was willing to move to Majorca so that John could paint. He would even try to contact the noted English poet Robert Graves, who lived there and might mentor Philip in writing. He certainly would love to live in Majorca, their paradise.

In times of distress, Philip turned to his Catholic faith. He prayed but got no answer from God, so he decided to speak with Father Michael, the Catholic chaplain on the base. Philip had never had any contact with this priest, but since he represented Christ on earth, Philip would seek guidance from him.

When he entered the chaplain's quarters, the space almost reminded him of the sacristy of his church at home. He thought he should begin by making his confession, but there was no confessional booth with a screen between the priest and the penitent; there were only two chairs opposite each other. Philip had to look into the eyes of the chaplain as he related his story.

He said, "Father Michael, I would like to talk to you about a serious matter. Do you think I should go to confession first, although it's been a long time?"

Father Michael replied, "Let's discuss your important matter first."

"Well, I don't know where to begin."

"Just begin with the present situation."

"I am truly in love for the first time in my life. Love and sex have always been separate for me, but this is the first time I have found them together."

"That's wonderful. Is she German?"

"I have fallen in love with another soldier."

"That can't be. How did that happen?"

"I don't know. I've had sex with men before, but I never loved them. Then a couple times in college and in acting class in New York, I did fall in love, but they were straight, so there wasn't any sex."

"My son," said Father Michael—these words sounded strange to Philip, since he was only a few years younger than the priest—"it's not real love. It is just lust. It is the devil tempting you."

His words stung. Philip wished he had had the strength when he was in college to confide in one of the priests there. They had been so understanding and sympathetic. But in the atmosphere of the 1950s, it had not been easy to speak with anyone about homosexuality.

"But Father, I do love John. I feel that God has sent him to me. I always wonder how God created a man so beautiful on the outside and inside. He is everything I have always wanted."

"Is he Catholic?"

"Yes."

"Then he knows it's a sin. His soul will go to hell."

"How can it be a sin when we love each other so much?"

"You both have been away from your families. You have been lonely, so you seek each other out."

"I have been lonely most of my life, but I've never found anyone to love like this."

"You must not see him anymore!"

"I'll die without him."

"That is the devil putting these ideas in your mind. Have you had sex with him?"

"Yes."

"What do you do?"

"Do I have to go into detail?"

"Yes. You must confess every sexual act."

"We kiss and caress each other."

"What else do you do?"

"We have oral sex."

"Do you put your penis in his mouth? Does he put his penis in yours?"

"Yes."

"It is the work of the devil. What else?"

"We have intercourse."

"Do you mean you put your penis in his rectum? And he sticks his into your rectum?"

"Yes."

"Disgusting—and sinful. You must atone for your sins and hope that he does the same. The devil has tempted you both. You must not see each other, and you must mend your ways. What did it feel like when he put his penis in you?"

"Oh, uh, my body ... my body tingled all over. I felt like he was pouring his love into me. I don't care if I go to hell, but I cannot condemn his soul to hell."

"That is what you will do if you continue to see him."

"Can I just be his friend?"

"No. The temptation will be too great, and the devil will win out."

"Okay, Father. I will try."

"Feel free to come see me whenever you are tempted to sin again," said Father Michael, putting his hand on Philip's thigh.

Philip cringed, since he could not help but see a growing mound in Father Michael's crotch.

"We will work things out," said the priest. "Go in peace, my son."

Philip was conflicted. The priest had caused him to fear for John's soul. Philip did not care if he himself was condemned to hell, but he felt that he must save John. He suggested that they go to a gasthaus near the post, a simple gasthaus where none of the soldiers would go. He and John could drink beer and be left alone.

Although he was only a few years older than John, he felt he had a lifetime more of experience. Sitting at the table, waiting for their beers to be brought to them, Philip said, "I think you should go back to college when you go home to California."

John said, "I will go to college if you really want me to."

Philip continued, "I also think you should see a psychiatrist to discuss what we've been doing."

John replied, "I don't know if that will make any difference, but I'll go if you want me to."

Philip pressed on. "You've been away from American girls for so long that maybe you should see what it would be like to go out with them again."

"I know what it is like. I have gone out with them. I know you want me to do these things, but I really want to get discharged and stay here and live in Anna's house. We could save enough money to go to Majorca."

Then Philip said he had to go to the bathroom. As he stood at the urinal, feeling a buzz as he urinated, he remembered a movie in which Ingrid Bergman told her lover she didn't love him anymore, in order to save his life. He couldn't remember any other details, but he could remember her deceiving her lover in a convincing way.

When he returned to the table, he told John, "I have to tell you something. I don't know quite how to tell you this, but I'm not in love with you anymore."

Stunned, John said, "I don't believe you."

"It's true. I don't know how it happened, but I just don't want to have sex with you. I still like you as a friend, but that other part has died."

"Why are you saying this? Does it have something to do with your talk with the chaplain?"

"No. This is just the way I feel now." Philip felt relieved that he would no longer be responsible for John's soul.

John looked as if he were halfway convinced—and hurt.

They walked back to the post in silence. When they entered their room, even though he knew it was dangerous, John gently kissed Philip and led him to his bed and said, "We always do it on your bed. This time I would like to do it on my bed."

"But I don't want to do it anymore," Philip said feebly.

John ignored this and continued to kiss and undress him.

Philip cried out, "Oh, I do love you. I can't help it."

John lay head to toe with him and made love to him. Philip reciprocated automatically. He had the most intense orgasm of his life and flooded John's mouth with ejaculation after ejaculation. Afterward, they held each other as tears flowed from both of them.

"You didn't mean what you said before, did you?" pleaded John.

"No. No. I'll never stop loving you," Philip said. "But I do think you need to go back home and work a few things out, and then I will join you there."

For the most part, what happened in the outside world had had little impact on their daily lives on the base. But while they were living in their private world and looking forward to being discharged from the army in a few months, events were taking place in the rest of the world that would have a profound effect on their lives.

In April 1961, President John F. Kennedy ordered the implementation of a plan he had inherited from President Dwight D. Eisenhower, one that had been drawn up by the CIA and the US military to assist a group of anti-Castro Cubans in an invasion of Cuba to bring down Fidel Castro. Kennedy gave the order despite having serious doubts about the plan. His doubts were justified. The plan, which came to be known as the Bay of Pigs Invasion, was a great failure. It emboldened Castro to declare war on "rock 'n' roll" and to send priests and gays to labor camps.

In Germany in 1961, the Cold War was in full swing. First, the Russians forbade travel between East and West Berlin because so many of their best men and women were defecting; then they began to erect a "wall" of barbed-wire fence. President Kennedy met with Nikita Khrushchev in Vienna in June and attempted to negotiate, but the confrontation in Germany continued.

On July 25, 1961, President Kennedy ordered Congress to appropriate $3 billion more for the military, to triple the draft, to call up the reserves, and to extend the tour of duty of draftees already serving in the military.

John, who had enlisted, had already begun his discharge process and would receive his discharge papers before the extension took effect. But Philip, who had been drafted, was caught by the extension and would have to serve an additional four months past his September discharge date, so he would not be free until January 1962. He hoped the conflict would be resolved quickly and his extra months in the military would be canceled.

On August 13, 1961, East Germany's Communist rulers ordered the closure of the borders and began erecting a wall—a real wall, almost twelve feet high, made of concrete—between East and West Berlin.

It happened on a Sunday morning, when the troops normally could sleep late. However, on that Sunday morning they were awakened early, to be told about the wall in Berlin and to be informed that if the Russian troops invaded Germany, they would have seven minutes to live before the Russians bombed all the American posts. The soldiers were also told not to worry if the Russians destroyed everybody, because there were troops in America ready to take their place.

As it turned out, the Berlin Wall was erected without

incident. American troops stayed on the western side of Berlin and the Russians on the eastern side. Life on the post returned to normal. But the wall reinforced the need for the presence of American troops in Germany and meant that there was no possibility of Philip's extra months of service being shortened.

Philip was in such despair over the extension of his tour of duty that he threatened to jump off the three-story building that housed the office of the commanding officer, but it made no difference. In fact, the executive officer just laughed and said they would keep him there forever.

Philip and John's life plans had been thrown into disarray. They were horrified by this credo of war—that people who didn't know you or care about you could influence the course of your life and could even send you to your death. Now John was about to go home to California, and Philip was stuck in Germany for six more months.

Philip knew the best escape from this madness would be a trip to the dentist, who had the reputation of being the most pleasant and caring officer on the post. Soldiers soon learned that if they went to him with "a headache from a toothache," he would give them Miltown, a mild tranquilizer affecting the nervous system. In the 1950s and early 1960s, it was prescribed heavily for people in America for the treatment of anxiety. It also produced a great calming effect on the troops, reducing outbursts of anxiety that could result in insubordination and fights.

In the seclusion of his room, Philip took a couple of Miltowns and lay down to take a nap and escape into oblivion.

Fifteen

A Dream Life

"Come on, lazy bones," teased John, tickling him.
"We have to move my stuff to our room in Anna's house before
there is too much traffic in town."

Surprised, Philip asked, "Did you finish your discharge
papers already?"

"I paid off a few of the guys to get to the front of the line
so we could get out of here as soon as possible. I can't wait to
set up my things in our home."

They packed all John's things to add to his possessions
that were already in Anna's house. Because Philip had to
remain on the post for a few more months, they didn't take
any of his gear.

Anna greeted them with a loving welcome. This would
now be their permanent home, not just a place where they
could escape from the army. She provided them with more
dishes and cooking utensils, so they had very little to buy to
complete their home. As soon as she left, they got naked and
lay on the bed. They embraced as if they could be absorbed
into each other's body by osmosis.

John immediately went into town to find a job so that he could begin saving money for their move to Majorca. He asked the jeweler who had made Philip's gold ring if he needed a designer. The jeweler was thrilled to have an American artist and quickly gave him some assignments; he welcomed the American and especially the Californian perspective that John could bring to the more traditional designs of German jewelry.

With John's income and unemployment check and Philip's army pay, they figured they could move to Majorca in a few months. Philip just enjoyed living a normal civilian life when he visited John in their room, choosing not to think of the awful return to the post that would come at the end of the visit. Now he lived alone in his room on the base, and he preferred the loneliness to the annoyance of military chatter from another soldier.

Any night that Philip could get a pass to be with John, he walked down the mountain path, which was covered with shimmering leaves. Every novel and poem that he had read came to life. The beauty was no longer on the page but in Philip's being. His creative thoughts had come to life in his union with John.

Philip wrote to Robert Graves through his publisher in London and discovered that Mr. Graves had accepted a post as a professor at Oxford. They corresponded for a while, and eventually, Mr. Graves wrote Philip that he wanted to help him and his friend John. He himself had been seriously wounded in World War I and had almost died, so he had a special place in his heart for military men. He sensed that John was a "special" friend and said he had also had an intimate relationship with a man before he married. He offered his house in Deià, Majorca, with plenty of room for them, at no charge. The caretaker had instructions to make them comfortable there for as long as they wished. He signed off, hoping that he would meet them one day to exchange stories.

John also wrote to Picasso's agent and received an invitation to visit Picasso when he would be with his group of artists in Vallauris. It seemed that these accomplished people had an interest in and a willingness to help the US soldiers.

When Philip was discharged, he and John had a tearful farewell party with George, Philomena, Jim, and Damian. Then they took the train to Stuttgart to have an intimate farewell party with Ann and Judy.

They took several trains that eventually delivered them to Antibes in the South of France, where Picasso lived. Then they took a bus the short distance to Vallauris, where Picasso had given new life to the town with his ceramic work. He had established a retreat for various artists, writers, poets, photographers, actors, and musicians from around the world. Philip and John immersed themselves in this world of artistry for three days of intellectual stimulation—the farthest one could get from the military life.

Then it was on to paradise: Majorca. The train to Barcelona and the boat to Majorca filled them with joy. Mr. Graves had provided comprehensive directions to his stone villa, which had a Roman arch doorway. As they approached the villa, the sun cast an orange-red glow on it. They felt a force pulling them toward their new home; they felt as if they had lived here in another life.

A gentle old man appeared to guide them to their room. He revealed that he was the caretaker and was there to grant their every wish. At the moment their only wish was to sleep after their long trip.

They awoke to the orange-red sun blazing as if it had never

set. The stone house had retained a comfortable coolness, and when they stepped outside, the rays of the sun energized them. On a table with an umbrella, a lovely breakfast was set out for them. After they were completely filled, they asked the caretaker if he had any chores they could do. He gave them a corner of the garden where they could plant vegetables for themselves. They could also plant flowers to adorn their room.

John designed the garden layout to accommodate both flowers and vegetables. As Philip began digging holes for the seeds, he said, "It feels good to work with the earth. When I was growing up, my father planted tomatoes. He wouldn't let me help with the planting, but he allowed me to pick the ripe tomatoes. It is my fondest memory of him."

John said, "My father let me clean the horse shit in the stable. All he cared about were those damn horses. I guess there were some good times when I went riding with him."

They took off their shirts to get a tan as they worked. When they were nearly finished, Philip stared at John's chest and said, "I can't stand it any longer. I have to have you. Let's go to the room."

John eagerly followed him. The old man smiled as he saw them rushing to the house.

Making love in their new home was a joy unparalleled. They could create their own world while also being a part of the real world. The integration of mind, body, and soul was accomplished.

Philip whispered, "I know that you will always be a part of me, no matter what happens to us in life."

"And you'll always be in my heart," replied John. "I never knew I could feel this way with someone. I had girlfriends and had sex with them but always felt something was missing. I didn't know what. Now I know—it was you."

Their days were filled with painting for John and writing for Philip. John painted the fascinating olive trees and sometimes portraits of Philip, who was writing a play about the army.

When John took his paintings to a local gallery, the owner told him that Joan Miró was living in Palma; his wife was from there. Miró had a group of apprentices and students who aspired to be as great an artist as he. He worked with them in a three-hundred-year-old house that he had bought for that purpose. Although John didn't know much about Miró's work, he discovered that the artist's inspiration was Van Gogh, whom John worshiped. The gallery owner called Miró to ask if John could join them, and Miró said yes. John couldn't wait to tell Philip the good news.

Philip was ecstatic for John and also for himself. It was difficult for Philip to write with John interrupting and tempting him. When John was at Miró's studio, Philip would be able to write undisturbed by his attraction for John. Now they both could work in peace and satisfy their desires at night.

Philip continued corresponding with Robert Graves, who by now had become his mentor, even though it was at a distance. Graves told him that Graves's early drafts of *I, Claudius* were in his desk if Philip cared to read them. Philip studied them and saw the progression and development of this great novel. He was learning from Graves through his writings.

One evening John seemed unusually vulnerable. Philip was very tender toward him and cuddled him. As the orange-red sun sank into the sea, a blue-gray mist filled Philip's field of vision.

SIXTEEN

The Farewell

As the blue-gray mist cleared, Philip woke up and found himself in his room on the base. Completely disoriented, he tried to comprehend what had happened. Suddenly, he realized that he had been dreaming about being discharged and staying in Europe with John.

Then reality hit him. He had convinced John to go back to the United States. He ran down the stairs to the quad, where John was preparing to leave the post.

The army truck was parked in front of headquarters with the back flap open. Soldiers were rushing out of the building with their discharge papers, ecstatic to be leaving and going home. Philip stood on the gravel pavement and looked at John, who was standing in the back of the truck. John looked confused. He was not ecstatic about going.

Philip was paralyzed. He felt as if there was so much air in his chest, and yet he could not breathe. The air created emptiness that rose to his head. He could not hear the shouts of joy from the other soldiers; he just heard the silence between him and John. He moved his lips, but no words emerged. He tried to walk closer to the truck, but his feet would not move. The emptiness created a longing that could not be filled. When he felt wetness on his cheeks, he realized it was from tears. The motor of the truck was revving up, causing his heart to grab at his throat. All the while, he and John looked directly into each other's eyes. The message was conveyed without words. Philip saw the tears in John's eyes as he slumped against the wooden side of the truck.

Philip's paralysis was penetrated by a loud noise, and the truck began to move away, pulling the life from Philip's heart and causing pain in his head, chest, stomach, crotch, legs, and feet. The truck faded into the distance, and Philip swayed back and forth.

"Hey, it looks like you're going to fall over," his captain said, catching him before he could hit the ground.

"I just felt a little faint, but I'm okay now," Philip said. He turned toward the barracks and began a dead man's walk. He knew he had made a terrible mistake that would change his life forever. Why had he told John to leave? Who did he think he was? Just because he had a degree in psychology, he thought he knew what was best for John?

Philip found it hard to believe that at twenty-three his life was over. He prayed that John would begin a new life to save his soul. But how was Philip going to live now, without John?

Right now he had to walk to his office in the barracks. He was able to move and place one foot in front of the other, automatically. He could navigate across the courtyard to his office in his sleep. He did not require any feeling in his empty body to get there. The only thought he could sustain was his destination—his office.

When Philip entered the office, his gray, drained face

caused his commanding officer to exclaim, "You don't look so good. Why don't you take the rest of the day off?"

"Okay, sir," moaned Philip, as he turned and headed for the stairway to his room.

He entered the room and was hit with the reality that John was never coming back to the bunk opposite his. It was empty and would be for the rest of his life. There was no reversing his decision. There was no undoing it. He had not thought it through and had never expected to be dealt this blow. Now his life would only be time to kill. He lay in his bunk and waited for death to come.

Seventeen

Where to Go?

Philip would be alone in Germany for four more months. How was he going to survive without John? All of his close friends, including George, Philomena, Jeremiah, and Sheldon, and even his new friend Damian, had already been discharged.

He desperately looked for someone to whom he could relate. Then he met Albrecht, who had been born in Vienna and had joined the US Army so he could become an American citizen. He had a sense of humor similar to Philip's, and his slight Viennese accent added color to his amusing remarks about everything.

Philip yearned to have Albrecht's strong arms encircle him, to have a chest and stomach press into him, to have legs wrapped around his, to have a human body he could touch. There was only air for him to grasp now. He looked at men as if he had no right to them. He was on an island by himself and never would be able to hug and squeeze and press against another body.

This longing for another man to hold had surfaced when

he met Albrecht. The link that had brought them together was the theater. Albrecht wanted to be an actor too. In his case the desire was understandable, since his mother was a famous actress and his father a famous director in Vienna. Philip clung to his theater friend as a beacon in the stormy waters of the army.

Since Albrecht spoke perfect German, they could explore uncharted parts of Schwäbisch Gmünd. Philip was excited by these adventures until he realized that John was not there to enjoy them with him. No matter how wondrous an experience might be, in Philip's mind there was always the specter of John, accompanying him like a ghost.

Thanksgiving without his friends was uneventful, but then Christmas approached. Memories of the previous year's wonderful Christmas with John flooded Philip's senses, rendering him physically weak and vulnerable.

He dragged himself around the base, performing his duties as if he were a robot. The cold weather sent a chill through his body, and he began to run a fever. The doctor prescribed a couple of days of bed rest.

Albrecht visited him in his room. "I know the cure for what ails you. I know just what you need," he announced. "I'll take you home to Vienna with me for Christmas. You have two weeks of leave coming up, and there is no better way to spend it than with my family."

Philip wasn't sure if he would be well enough to make the journey, but he decided that if he could go to Vienna, then he also could go on to Rome and spend Christmas with his friend Susan from acting class in New York; she was in Rome, hoping to get into a movie.

When the time came to leave Germany, he pulled himself together. He felt a twinge of excitement at the thought of going to Vienna and meeting Albrecht's parents, who were stars in the theater.

When Philip and Albrecht arrived in Vienna, the city was elegantly decked out for Christmas, with crystal lights and giant chandeliers lighting up the night sky. Crowds flocked to the Christmas markets, which sold everything imaginable, from Christmas decorations to gingerbread, jars of jam, and hams. People stood in line at the food stands, which sold roasted chestnuts and potatoes or sausages, and in line for *Weihnachtspunsch* served in mugs. Philip loved the vintage ornaments made from handblown glass and ceramics, a startling contrast to decorations in America, which were mostly made of plastic. Beeswax candles lit many establishments, producing an old-world charm that seemed to wrap its arms around Philip.

Albrecht's family welcomed him with warm holiday cheer. They wanted to hear about his life in America and were especially interested in the Actors Studio in New York; they thought Marlon Brando was the most exciting actor. They had been trained in the Max Reinhardt Studio, in a more classical method. Philip explained some of the Method exercises to help the actor portray a character more realistically. They were going to try the exercises in their acting classes to see if they could incorporate this technique into their acting skills.

They discussed many topics, from the rococo architecture Philip was interested in to the Spanish Riding School. Philip told them, "I saw the Lipizzan horses perform in Madison

Square Garden when they were in New York. I had never seen anything like them!"

Albrecht's mother said, "They are not performing while you are here, but I can get permission for you to visit the stables."

This was a treat he hadn't expected. Albrecht took him first to the palace, where the horses typically performed in a large rectangular room with a rug on the floor and crystal chandeliers hanging from the ceiling. Then to the stables they went, to the inner sanctum of the Spanish Riding School. The stables were spotless, and Philip noted the lack of odor. Stalls lined either side of a long aisle. The horses in those stalls were pure white, although they had been born black. Philip pointed out the huge erections on many of the stallions. Albrecht laughed and told Philip he had better get him out of there before he got any ideas.

Albrecht's mother was starring in a play that his father was directing at the Burgtheater Wien. Albrecht had a previous engagement, so he took Philip to the theater early to leave him with the stage manager.

They entered the theater through the stage door, where the stage manager met them. He was happy to show Philip around. First, he took Philip backstage to see the revolutionary revolving stage. It rotated on a cylinder and was so efficient that the scenery could be changed in less than a minute. Then the stage manager took him out into the house, and Philip marveled at the two imperial staircases, which had been painted by Gustav Klimt and his brother Ernst. The rococo architecture was certainly different from the style of Broadway theaters.

Just before curtain time, the stage manager escorted Philip to a box seat. There were several unoccupied seats in the box, which was a bit disconcerting to Philip. He noticed many people in the auditorium looking up at him, sitting there alone. He felt intimidated and was thankful when the curtain went up.

He was thrilled to see Albrecht's mother onstage. She played her part beautifully. The audience gave her an overwhelming ovation that required several curtain calls. Philip went backstage to see her. She was very appreciative of his comments and held him as if he were part of the family—and he did feel a sense of belonging in this foreign theater. When she took him to meet the other actors in a café nearby, they acted as if he were the star, since he was from New York. They too wanted to hear about the Actors Studio and the modern techniques that he had shown Albrecht's mother. He was surprised since they were part of the Max Reinhardt Studio, which had operated for a hundred years, but it pleased him that he could contribute something meaningful.

When Philip returned to Albrecht's house after the play, his friend greeted him at the door with a knowing smile. "Well, how was your evening?"

"How did you do that? Get me a private box? It was incredible! Why were people staring at me?"

Albrecht laughed. "Because you were sitting in the president's box."

"Oh my God!" exclaimed Philip. "And your mother is so wonderful."

"She arranged a lot of these things for you," admitted Albrecht. "I hoped this trip would cheer you up. I know how upset you've been over John leaving."

"You know how close we were?"

"Yes," said Albrecht sympathetically as he put his arms around Philip.

Philip was startled. He hadn't been touched since John left. Albrecht led Philip to his bedroom.

"Let's go to bed," said Albrecht, and he took off all his clothes.

Philip tried not to stare as he followed suit and removed all his clothes.

They got into a double European bed, which was not very large. They both lay on their backs and occasionally touched each other's arms and legs. Philip tried to fall asleep and not move, but he was agitated by the presence of this beautiful and kind man. He started to get an erection when he thought Albrecht had fallen asleep. Suddenly, Albrecht turned toward him and threw his left leg over him, placing his crotch on top of Philip's. Philip was puzzled by this behavior and didn't make a move toward Albrecht. He thought, *I must be dreaming.* Then he felt Albrecht's erection pushing into his penis. Philip spontaneously put his arms around Albrecht and ground his penis into him.

"What are you doing?" screamed Albrecht, jumping up.

"I was just reacting to you," Philip said fearfully.

"I was dreaming. But I think that this Austrian wine has gone to your head. You better not drink anymore."

Philip apologized and tried to sleep, but he couldn't close his eyes until the sunrise. He was grateful that he was scheduled to leave for Rome that day, but he couldn't stop worrying about Albrecht, about how he would react when they were back at the army base. Albrecht drove him to the train station and bade him farewell. He was as cheerful as ever and didn't mention the previous night.

Philip was looking forward to seeing Susan again. She and another actor Philip knew slightly were living in Rome, trying to get parts in the movie *Cleopatra*; filming had dragged on for months due to Elizabeth Taylor's illnesses.

Susan met Philip at Stazione Termini in Rome. They

hadn't seen each other for two years, and they fell into a happy embrace. They took a taxi to her pensione, where she had reserved a room for him. She told him the latest gossip from New York and about how their former mutual acting partner, Barbra Streisand, was becoming a singing star.

Philip asked Susan, "Can we go to the Café de Paris?" It was on the Via Veneto and was the spot where *La Dolce Vita* had been filmed.

Susan agreed, and it was fun for both of them to sit in the café and watch the characters parade by.

There was an exclusive men's store across from where they sat. "I want to buy a tie for Albrecht," Philip told Susan, "to show him how much I appreciate his taking me to Vienna to see his family."

"It will be expensive," Susan warned.

Philip told her, "No matter what it costs, it won't suffice for what Albrecht did for me in Vienna."

They walked across the street, and he found just the right tie and bought it.

When Susan saw that it cost the equivalent of fifty dollars, she was upset at such extravagance. "How could you spend that much money on a tie?" She and her actor friend had been living on next to nothing in order to stay in Rome until they got acting jobs.

Philip tried to explain. "Being in the army, I don't have to pay living expenses. I have enough money to spend on a friend, you included."

Susan still was not happy about it. When they met for supper that night, she told him that she had to go to a party with her American actor friend.

When her friend arrived, Philip immediately disliked him

because he said, "In order to be an actor, you have to be a prostitute."

"Is it a party with people in the movie business?" Philip asked.

"No, just people from Brazil that he just met," Susan answered.

"It's Christmas Eve, so I thought we could go to Midnight Mass—maybe at Saint Peter's Basilica," Philip suggested.

"I have to go to the party. I'm sorry I can't invite you to go with me," Susan said.

"That's all right," a stunned Philip replied.

When she left, he felt so lonely that he knew he had to return to Germany to be with Anna's family. That was the closest he could get to John, since Anna had been their landlady. He quickly packed and took a taxi to the train station. The dark and dreary streets were deserted. On the sidewalk sat a poor woman holding her baby. He thought about the *Madonna with Child*. The baby held out his hand, and Philip crammed into his little hand all the Italian money he had.

The woman cried thankfully. "O Dio, Dio," she said.

Philip rushed to the train, trying to see through his tears.

Anna was happy to see him, and her five-year-old granddaughter jumped into his arms. Philip was through feeling sorry for himself. He had a genuine family who loved him. He would not seek love anywhere else.

He wrote more often to John, but John's letters became more infrequent. Philip planned to go to California as soon as he got discharged. He hoped John still loved him.

Eighteen

Reentry into the Real World

At last Philip was discharged. Albrecht promised to keep in touch with him, since he planned to live in New York City someday. Philip was happy that their friendship had withstood the incident in Vienna. He did want Albrecht to be his friend and looked forward to seeing him in New York.

The ocean was so rough on the trip to New York that Philip lost count of how many times he threw up. Army ships were not meant for comfort. He thought about his father, at the age of twelve, coming with his family from Italy in third class. They all had gotten very sick but had made it to the "promised land." If they could do it, he also could do it.

He had never before been so happy to see the Statue of Liberty, although he couldn't stay in New York City. He had to take a train to see his family upstate. They cried with relief that he had made it back safely. It was a great comfort, more than he had imagined, to be with his family. He didn't want to dampen their spirits, so he did not tell them about his broken heart; he also hoped to mend it by going to California to see John as soon as he could.

After a couple of weeks, he informed his parents that he was going to California to try to get into the movies, and again he did not tell them about John. They were saddened that he was leaving, but they knew he had been a serious acting student and tried to understand his desire to have a career in show business. He returned to New York City, planning to take a nonstop flight to Los Angeles in a couple of days.

Philip had heard that Susan had returned to New York City too, but he didn't know how to contact her. Their friend Barbra was performing in the musical comedy *I Can Get It for You Wholesale.* The show was trying out in Philadelphia and would soon move to Broadway. Philip thought Barbra might know where Susan was living, since Susan had often brought Barbra to Philip's apartment on West Forty-Fourth Street when they all had been in Eli Rill's acting class, before Philip had been drafted into the army.

Hoping to see Susan before he left New York to go to California, Philip wondered if he should go to Philadelphia and find Barbra, to see if she could tell him anything about Susan. But he also knew how fate could play tricks and turn everything around in one day, so instead he decided to go to California as soon as possible. Philip phoned John in California to let him know he was on the way.

John and a friend picked Philip up at the Los Angeles airport. As they were leaving, a police car pulled up beside them, and the police wanted to see Philip's identification and inspect his luggage. It was an unexpected way to be welcomed to Los Angeles and reminded Philip of surprise army inspections. He passed the police inspection, although he was shaken by it.

The next surprise in store for Philip was that rather than going to John's apartment, they spent the night in his friend's home, and John was not intimate with Philip. Philip didn't know how to react. He had thought they would find an apartment and live together, but John informed him that he would have to find a place of his own. Philip wanted to be independent but was confused by John's not inviting him to stay with him.

The next day, they looked for a furnished apartment that Philip could afford with his savings and unemployment checks. They found one near Hollywood and Vine, an ideal location for Philip, since he did not have a car. He would be able to walk to many places, an unheard-of behavior in Hollywood, or take public transportation. The apartment was in a two-story motel surrounding a rectangular grass courtyard. The motel's big claim to fame was that Anita Ekberg had stayed there when she first came to Hollywood. The apartment had shabby furniture, but it was clean. John told him that the apartment was as nice as his.

Philip, who had counted on John's companionship, was now forced to be on his own. He knew he would need money and immediately went to register at the unemployment office. Culture shock set in right then, when the actress Terry Moore pulled up in a chauffeured limousine to collect her unemployment check.

Philip knew he wasn't in New York anymore and would have to learn the customs of this strange land. Everything in Los Angeles was so different from New York. The buildings looked as if they had been built yesterday and would fall apart tomorrow. He soon learned that even the palm trees had been imported. One night when he was out walking, he saw dozens of palm trees lying in the gutter, lining the street. "What happened to them?" he asked a man he passed on the sidewalk.

"Oh, nothing. They have just been imported, and they are all lined up, ready to be planted tomorrow," the person told him.

Philip knew he had to find a job to lengthen the time he could collect unemployment, and John finally told him they needed another person in his office, where they did credit checks for people who wanted a mortgage. Philip interviewed and got the job. He and John worked different shifts, so they never saw each other at work. Philip felt disappointed and disoriented and didn't dare approach John, but he still hoped that they could have a private conversation soon.

In the course of investigating people's credit, Philip came across a woman who had the same last name as him—Mary Greco. He asked her if she had relatives in Syracuse, where his family lived. She told him that part of her family had gone to New York State, but she had lost track of them.

She told him, "I do the costumes for the TV show *Bonanza*."

Philip said, "I'm an actor, and I always watch the show." After he gave her a good credit rating for her mortgage, she invited him to the set. Although he wasn't the Western type, and there would never be a part for him on the show, he was excited to see his first professional television show being filmed. The cast and crew were very familiar with each other and had a great time filming. A goat peed on the set and caused a roar of laughter in the middle of a scene.

When they finished, Michael Landon, who played Little Joe, offered Mary a ride home in his limo. She told him, "Philip is my guest."

Michael said, "Bring him along. There's plenty of room."

So all three piled into the back seat, along with several other cast members. Philip had to practically sit on Landon's lap.

"Don't be bashful. You can sit on my lap."

Philip grew weak because he thought Michael was so handsome and personable. They let Philip out at his apartment, and he was ecstatic over his moment in the real Hollywood.

John haunted Philip's thoughts. Eventually, Philip felt so desperate to talk with him that he worked up the nerve to invite him to dinner at his apartment, where they wouldn't be disturbed and could at last have a chance to talk privately.

In Germany, Philip had told John to do three things when he got back to America: see a psychiatrist to discuss his sexuality, go back to college, and date girls.

When he came over for dinner, John said, "I went to a psychiatrist, and he told me I didn't need therapy. I enrolled at the university, but I didn't like the classes, so I dropped out. And I'm now dating American girls. So I did everything you asked me to do."

Philip asked, "Don't you think we should live together?"

John answered, "It wouldn't be a good idea. We're not like the homosexual guys in Los Angeles."

"I know we're not."

John said, "We can't act like that here."

"What do you mean?" Philip asked.

"For example, the way we walk. I bought boots to make me look more masculine. You should too."

"We walked the same way in Europe."

"We can't be labeled homosexuals here in Los Angeles," demanded John.

"Do we have to have labels? Can't we just be us?"

"Other people would give us labels. It wouldn't be good for

our careers. You could be blacklisted, and no one in the movie business would hire you."

"You come first for me," Philip argued.

"You say that now, but if we were labeled, you might feel different."

"I still love you."

"I love you too, but not in that way," John said.

"How could that have changed?"

"It just is different."

"I'm scared, John."

"Don't be. You'll find your way here."

"I only came because of you," Philip pleaded.

"Don't say that. You can't depend on me. You have to find your own way."

"You're breaking my heart," Philip said.

"I'm sorry."

"No one will ever love you the way I do."

"How can you say that?" John asked.

"I just know it. I'll love you forever."

"I have to go."

Philip felt as if he were falling into a dark abyss. After all they had been through in the army, he had thought that once they were out, they would live together in freedom forever. He felt the sensation of being out of his body and looking down on himself, far from home, lying in a bed that was not his, in an apartment that had been designed for someone else. How could he ever live alone in this strange land?

He had made a mistake.

When they were in Germany, Jim had wanted to live with Philip, but he had chosen John instead. He felt that he was always pursuing John. With Jim it had been different. Jim had always wanted him, always wanted to make love to him.

He remembered how Jim had begged him to let him know whenever he was free, so they could make love.

On one occasion in the army, John and Philip, although estranged, had gone together to visit Aloysius and his wife in their new apartment in Schwäbisch Gmünd. After one drink Philip had announced that he had a date and had to leave. That didn't seem strange to the others, because they didn't know that he and John had been lovers as well as roommates. John knew that Philip was going to see Jim, but he said nothing and continued to drink.

When Philip arrived at his and John's room, he found Jim waiting there, completely nude. Jim grabbed Philip as soon as he entered and kissed him as he removed Philip's clothes.

"I was afraid you wouldn't come," exclaimed Jim.

"I promised you. John doesn't want to make love, so why shouldn't I come to you?"

Jim said, "What did John say when you left? I don't want to come between you, but I do love you."

"John said nothing," Philip reassured him. "He just kept drinking. I don't think he cares."

Jim kissed him all over and took his penis into his mouth. As Philip moaned, Jim said, "I love to feel you in my mouth. Let's get an overnight pass and go to Stuttgart. We can get a hotel so we can make love all night."

"I have to go with John when I get an overnight," Philip said.

"Remember that he canceled the last time?"

"I know, but I still belong to him."

"Next time you get an overnight, if John won't go with you, I will."

Jim led Philip to the bunk. He lay on top of him and placed his penis between Philip's legs under his scrotum because he knew that was Philip's favorite position. He humped Philip until Philip came. Jim did not come that way, so Philip masturbated him as Jim kissed him.

After he came, Jim said, "Thank you."

Philip said, "I loved doing it to you."

Jim added, "I love you doing it to me too."

Another night Jim had desired him so much that he arrived at Philip's room and told him he had to show him something. John lay in his bunk reading as Jim and Philip left. Jim took him to a hidden staircase that led to the attic.

"I didn't even know there was an attic," Philip said.

"I found out when we had to store the old mattresses here. Lie down with me."

"What if someone comes?"

"No one ever comes here." Jim got on top of Philip and kissed him as he rubbed him all over. He said, "Please take it out. I want to suck you."

Philip said, "We can't. What if someone comes? What would we say?"

Jim said, "I don't care." He placed his erection on top of Philip's erection and pushed into him until they both came in their fatigues. Jim said, "I love you so much. I just want to make you feel good."

Philip replied, "I love you too, but I met John first, and I belong to him. I have to stay with him."

"I know. I just want to be with you whenever you're free. I can wait," said Jim as he kissed him so deeply that the world faded for an instant.

Philip clung to Jim, but he had to get back to John.

Now, here in Los Angeles, John was ever more distant.

Nothing seemed real to Philip. Had he just imagined or dreamed that John had loved him so completely in the army? How could that love go away? Then he remembered that he had only dreamed that they had gone to live blissfully in Majorca; it had not happened. He also remembered how easy it had been to talk John into not staying in Germany when he got discharged.

Philip still had the Miltown the army doctor had prescribed for him. He lined the pills up on his bed and counted them—twenty-eight. That should do it.

Then he thought of all the reasons he should not commit suicide. His family would be devastated; they did not know about John and would not understand any of it. That would not help to get John back, so what was the purpose? To end the pain? From experience he had learned that no matter how severe, pain always subsided or was pushed into the background by time. Even though he was a Catholic, he was ambivalent about the sinfulness of suicide. Still, better to be safe than take a chance of going to hell. He put the pills back into the bottle and put the bottle in the medicine cabinet.

Philip walked out his door into the sunlit courtyard, with its green grass and fragrant flowers—which he couldn't have done in New York—and sat in the sun to get a tan. He lived on the ground floor, and there was another floor above him. This place reminded him just a little bit of his hometown, but the people were different. In fact, everything about the apartment complex seemed a little weird to him. Even the landlady was a character, maybe an alcoholic. However, there were some good-looking guys living in the motel. One of them, sitting across the courtyard, smiled at Philip and then got up and walked toward him.

"Hi, my name is Daniel," he said.

"Hi, I'm Philip."

"You're new here, aren't you?"

"Yes."

"I've been here six months. I'll show you the ropes."

"Oh, I'm an actor and came here to look for work."

"Yeah, sure. Everyone here is an actor. Do you have an agent or any connections?"

"No. I just have a friend who lives here."

"Boy, are you in for it. You better be careful of the vultures who will promise you everything so they can get into your pants."

"Oh, I wouldn't do that."

"Listen, after you're here awhile, you don't know what you'll do. I don't listen to promises anymore. I make them pay for sex. If they want to continue having it, then they have to give me a part."

"I don't think I have to worry about that, with all the hunks out here."

"Hey, you're a good-looking guy and innocent-looking. They like that. But you have to be discreet about it. They don't want anyone to know that they're gay. They're all hypocritical about it."

"Thanks for the advice."

"Listen, do you want to grill some steaks tonight?"

"I don't think I can afford that."

"Don't worry. I just turned a trick and have plenty of money. I'll get us some good steaks, and we can grill here in the courtyard. I promise I won't come on to you. I only do it for money now. Let's be friends."

"I really would like that. I'm feeling kind of lonely."

Philip's spirits were lifted by his new friend. Daniel

seemed to have a good heart, and Philip felt sad that he had to prostitute himself. Daniel seemed able to handle it, though, so maybe it wasn't bad for him. Philip knew he could never handle it.

However, their friendship was not destined to last long. Daniel soon found an agent who wanted him to move into his mansion in Beverly Hills. Daniel thought this was a fair exchange for fucking the agent every night.

✢

It was a while before Philip had an opportunity to make another friend. He got a small part in *Golden Boy* at an off-off-Broadway theater. He became friends with another serious actor, Carl, who was originally from Texas and had been on Broadway. Carl's wife Sharon was a nurse. They became his Hollywood family. They understood how heartbroken he was over John, and they often invited him to dinner. They made him feel he was always welcome.

John had a car and visited Philip once a week, though Philip could no longer fathom why he bothered. Sometimes they would drive out into the country. On one trip John brought his girlfriend, Christine, whom he called Chris. Philip thought it was fitting that John would call her a name that could also sound masculine. They attempted to convince Philip to go with them to the fundamentalist church that John had recently joined.

"You converted?" exclaimed Philip.

"Yes, Chris was a member, and she told me about it," explained John.

"What did your family say?" asked Philip.

"Oh, they flipped out. My mother was upset that I gave up

the Catholic religion, because she is so religious. My father disowned me, even though he's not such a great Catholic. When I told him Chris and I might get married, he really flipped out," answered John.

With a pain in his stomach, Philip said, "But you haven't known each other very long."

"I knew the first time I saw John that he was the one for me," Chris told Philip.

John said, "Do you know how much she loves me?" He demonstrated by picking his nose and putting his snot on her sleeve. "See, she lets me do anything to her."

Furious, Philip spat, "I think you're being pussy-whipped. She may have convinced you to join, but not me."

They didn't speak another word until they arrived at a country house on the beach in La Jolla. Philip learned that it belonged to Martin, a handsome, tall, blond young guy who was also pursuing John. John was certainly aware that Martin was gay, and it looked to Philip as if John liked the attention.

Philip had never seen this side of John before. As far as he knew, John had never thought of anyone in the army, other than Philip, as a lover. Now he seemed to love receiving attention from a gay male. And to top it all off, he was going to marry a girl he barely knew in a church he had hardly any knowledge of.

Overcome with emotion, Philip asked John to go sit in his car with him so they could have some privacy.

Philip asked, "Do you have sex with Christine?"

"Yes."

Philip continued, "Do you enjoy it?"

"Yes. It's different from the sex I had with you. It's not as intense, but it's satisfying."

Philip begged, "Can I kiss you? To see if you really have changed?"

"Okay, if you want to."

Philip tried to infuse the kiss with his love. Surprisingly, he felt nothing. He didn't know if he had changed or if he was so overpowered by the new John that their relationship had changed.

In desperation he went for a walk on the beach with Martin. When Martin said he had to pee, Philip realized he also had to relieve himself. They both walked to the water's edge and proceeded to urinate. Martin looked at Philip's penis and kissed him. Philip touched Martin in return. He wanted to have sex with this stranger, just to show John that other men were still interested in him. However, he lost his erection and couldn't follow through.

Philip realized that all he had was his acting career. He joined a class to immerse himself in the work. He participated as much as possible, doing improvisations and scenes. He developed a few friendships but nothing really meaningful.

Through the class he was able to get an interview with an agent. This would be his first professional entry into the world of Hollywood. It turned out that the agent, named Joseph, was from New York, and they immediately developed a rapport, discussing how much they missed the theater in New York. Joseph invited Philip out to dinner. Since Philip didn't have a car, the agent told him how to take a bus to his house and said he then would drive them to a restaurant.

When Philip arrived, he was impressed with the beautiful house. Joseph told him they would relax with his specialty drink before they went to the restaurant, and he went over to the well-stocked bar to make it. As Philip sat on the couch in the living room, he began to get nervous. He knew that the agent was legitimate because he had gotten a part for an actor whom Philip knew. Joseph returned with two drinks and sat very close to Philip. Philip tried to make conversation about his days in New York, but the agent kept moving closer and closer to him. As soon as they finished their drinks, the agent asked him if he would like to see his bedroom.

Philip was shocked and angry. "I thought you were serious," he said.

Joseph said, "I am serious. I think you have talent."

"So did you think I was so desperate that I would go to bed with you even before we had dinner?"

"I think you're very attractive. I thought you knew that I was attracted to you."

"Did you think that I would go to bed with you just to get a part?"

"I thought you would enjoy it too."

"Don't you have any self-respect? Don't you know that actors go to bed with you just to get a part?"

"I don't go to bed with every actor that I represent."

"Doesn't it bother you that even one actor would go to bed with you just to get a part?"

Joseph remained silent.

Philip said, "I'm hungry. I'll take you to dinner, and then you can drive me home."

Joseph agreed, and that is what he did. Of course, Philip never saw him again.

Philip knew that he could no longer bear to work in the same office where John worked. He asked to be laid off so that he could collect unemployment while he looked for another job.

Philip was not invited to John and Christine's wedding. The day they got married, Philip sat in his apartment watching television. He was distraught and couldn't imagine how he had gotten to this place, after the ecstasy he had experienced loving John. After a while he thought he smelled gas, but he couldn't be sure because he was in such a miserable state.

He kept thinking about the last time he had seen John, only a couple of weeks earlier. They had gone to the movies to see *The Children's Hour,* based on the play by Lillian Hellman. It was about two good friends, played by Audrey Hepburn and Shirley MacLaine, who run a private boarding school for girls. One evil girl tells her grandmother that she saw the two women kissing in Shirley MacLaine's bedroom. The scandal destroys the school. To prove her claim, the girl says she saw them through the keyhole in the bedroom door. When MacLaine states that there is no keyhole in the door, the evil child is exposed. Although they have been vindicated, MacLaine tells Hepburn that she does love her that way. Hepburn, in spite of not returning that love, asks MacLaine to go away with her to start afresh. Then Hepburn finds MacLaine hanging in her bedroom. Philip couldn't stop crying after the movie ended. He and John sat there until everyone had left the theater. John didn't say a word but drove Philip home.

Now the strong smell of gas jarred Philip out of his reverie. It seemed to be coming from his ceiling. He ran up to the apartment above him and banged on the door until a disheveled young woman answered it. Gas poured out of the apartment. Philip ran in, opened the windows, and turned off the stove, while the woman collapsed on her bed and cried.

"What happened?" asked Philip as he tried to comfort her.

"I want to die," she sobbed.

"Can you tell me about it?"

"I can't take it anymore. I thought that this time would be different. I thought he really loved me."

"I know how heartbreaking it is."

"Not only that, but he's going to live with a producer who promised to make him a star. And he'd never even had sex with a man before."

"Some people will do anything to become famous. My boyfriend left me for just the opposite reason. He didn't want to be famous but just wanted to get married and have kids."

"So you know how it feels?"

"Yes."

"How did you get over it?"

"I'm still trying to get over it. Will you come downstairs and have dinner with me? Maybe friends can help."

Fortunately, Philip did have some good friends. Carl and Sharon were always there for him. One Sunday they took him out to Malibu to a friend's home. It was a sunny day, and they had fun in the swimming pool. As they sat around the dinner table on the patio, someone said that Marilyn had killed herself.

"Who?" asked Philip.

"Marilyn Monroe. She finally did it."

"What a terrible thing to joke about."

"Who's joking? Haven't you listened to the radio?"

"No. What happened?"

"They found her early this morning with an empty bottle of sleeping pills."

Philip thought that he might be having a hallucination. These were people who knew her, and they were sitting around joking and laughing about her suicide. He excused himself from the table and went to the telephone. He called his parents, reversing the charges. When he heard his mother sobbing over Marilyn's death, he knew he wasn't going insane. But he could understand how Marilyn could kill herself in this crazy environment.

NINETEEN

Home at Mother's Balls

It was time to move out of the motel; Philip could no longer afford the rent. He found a cheaper apartment in a dreary building on Melrose Avenue in the shadow of Paramount Studios, so he could still dream about walking through the gates one day. It was humiliating not to be able to afford a decent apartment. This was the first time in his life he had been in this predicament. He tried not to think about how it would be if he could have lived with John.

The building did have a peculiar charm, even though it was in a poorer neighborhood in Los Angeles. The tenants seemed to be right out of a Tennessee Williams play. He felt a sense of security in being with the other denizens of the deep. They became his friends in their shared struggle to make it in Hollywood.

Barry, the first neighbor he met, happened to be an expat from New York. He was an aspiring photographer who was chubby and always smiling. He offered to take Philip's head-shots gratis. He also took Philip to dinner, since he had just received a check from his family. Philip didn't know if Barry was trying to seduce him, but he appreciated Barry's friendship and was entertained by his gossip.

Barry said, "I know everybody's story."

Philip asked, "What do you mean?"

"Well, wait until rent day. Then you can see Miss Yvette, in apartment 2A, in action. She claims to be an Arabian princess. She has a cute baby, Butchie, who doesn't have a father. Some creepy guy comes over once in a while to see the baby and claims to be the father. But I think he just comes over to fuck Miss Yvette."

Philip replied, "I have seen her, and she does look exotic."

Barry informed him, "She dresses that way because she can't afford decent clothes."

"You seem to have money. Why do you live here?" asked Philip.

"I love the atmosphere of the characters in this building," answered Barry. "Have you met the redhead in 2D, Deborah?"

"Yes, she's very attractive. Beautiful hair."

"Well, she claims to be an ex-showgirl from Las Vegas, but I think she's a prostitute. She came to Hollywood to be an actress. I don't see her doing much acting except with the men she brings up here. I love this place."

"Actually, I do feel at home here."

Once he had settled in, Philip answered an ad for a floral designer in a shop that sold artificial flowers, because the shop was nearby. The head designer, Donald, interviewed him.

Donald asked, "Have you worked in a florist shop before?"

Philip answered, "In New York. I had to cut the thorns off the roses that would be used in arrangements."

Donald asked, "Did you make arrangements?"

"No, I'm sorry," admitted Philip.

"That doesn't matter. The boss doesn't know anything

about arrangements. He just knows how to make money. We call him Gold Dick. I can teach you, so that's not a problem."

"I really would appreciate that. I just moved into an apartment near here."

"That's a plus. You will always be able to get here without worrying about the traffic on the freeways. The boss will like that."

It was interesting for Philip to meet the customers in the shop. Liberace and his brother came in to buy real-looking silk flowers to place in elegant vases on the piano next to the candelabra. The flowers were European and of the highest quality and would not wilt under hot studio lights the way real flowers would. Philip also helped Loretta Young's mother gather flowers that would be used on the set of *The Loretta Young Show*. Philip felt that he was at least in contact with show business, even if it was at a distance.

Of course, he knew nothing about doing floral arrangements, but that didn't matter in Hollywood. Fortunately, Donald had taken him under his wing and was very nurturing. Eric, the attractive designer, was considered the hot stud in the shop and was friendly toward him, but he did not respond to Philip's lust-filled advances. Instead, in a sisterly way, he told Philip about his sexual conquests. Almost everyone gravitated to him, even a twelve-year-old boy who was whisked away by his mother.

After Philip had been living in his house of the damned for a few months, Barry met Mac, who had no job and no money and who was happy to move into Barry's apartment. Mac would be the trashy white character in a Tennessee Williams play—he had long, stringy dirty-blond hair, a devilish look in his eyes, and a cruel mouth. He had a fairly muscular body and wore tight clothes to show everything, especially his penis. He looked like the typical hustler on Santa Monica Boulevard. In fact, that is where Barry had met him.

Now Barry had a lover. He was floating on air. The two of them included Philip when they went to the movies, Griffith Park, dinners, or any Hollywood event. Barry paid.

Miss Yvette cornered the three of them one day and said, "Are you the three musketeers?"

Philip replied, "Now I have someone to do things with."

"What kind of things?" asked Miss Yvette slyly.

"Not that kind," said Barry. "You have such a dirty mind!"

Miss Yvette had been living in the building for six months with her newborn son Butchie. One day when Jocko, the man who claimed to be the father, was there visiting, Miss Yvette told them that she was going to the store and he was taking care of Butchie.

Barry said, "I don't believe he's the father. He's a bum. He doesn't have a job or any money. He never brings anything for the kid."

Philip said, "Maybe Miss Yvette has to have a man that she can think is the father. No one else ever stays over."

"You always try to see the positive side," teased Barry.

Miss Yvette returned with her groceries. When she opened the door to her apartment, she screamed and threw the groceries at Jocko. She punched him as hard as she could while he was running out of the apartment. Philip and Barry ran to help her.

"What happened?" screeched Barry.

"The bastard was touching Butchie! He molested him!" she cried.

"The baby is smiling, and he's too young to know what happened. As long as he wasn't hurt physically, he'll be okay," said Philip as he picked him up. "He's too small to realize anything. He'll be all right."

Deborah heard the commotion and came out of her apartment. When she heard what had happened, she tried to comfort Miss Yvette. Their camaraderie was the saving grace for people living in such squalor; whenever anyone was hurting, they would all rally around that person.

Barry was ordered to return to New York for his father's birthday. He didn't mind this very much because it was also an opportunity for him to pick up some cash. He gave Mac money to live on while he was away. When he returned, Mac had found a different situation—he had moved in with Deborah. Barry discovered that Mac was bisexual when Deborah told him that she loved the way Mac "fucked."

Initially, Barry was upset, but he recovered quickly when he discovered he could still be friends with the newly formed couple. Once in a while, Mac fucked Barry to keep him satisfied. Deborah was very understanding. If Mac slept with her every night, he could fuck whomever he pleased. Philip tried to accept Mac as long as he made everyone happy.

Only Philip was not having regular sex. He was too depleted by his misery over John to have any desire. Occasionally, he would go to the gay bar and pick up a body. It almost didn't matter who it was as long as he got some release. However, these encounters never developed into a relationship.

While Philip was at an audition for a play to be directed by Ann-Margret's husband, Roger Smith, Carl and Sharon stopped by to see him. The building superintendent told them that he was out. They wrote a note to Philip that said, "We came by. Your super, Mother's Balls, told us you went to an audition." From then on, the one-eyed super—whose name was Motherall—was dubbed "Mother's Balls."

Rent day brought the oft-repeated ritual Barry had described when Philip first moved in. Whenever the super, Mother's Balls, went to Miss Yvette's apartment to collect the month's rent, Miss Yvette would rip her shirt open and run into the hallway screaming, "Rape! Rape! Call the police!" As expected, the super would run down the stairs and into his apartment as quickly as possible. All the tenants would come out of their apartments to congratulate Miss Yvette on her convincing performance. Once again, she would not have to pay that month's rent. In fact, on this latest occasion, none of the tenants on her floor, including Philip, had to pay rent. They all went out to dinner that night to celebrate their victory.

This was a new world for Philip. There was always something each day to help him ward off depression. One morning, his phone rang at eight, which was unusual.

"Hello," he groggily muttered.

"Philip, I need your help."

"Who is this?"

"It's Barry. I need you to call my father in New York."

"Where are you?"

"In jail."

"In jail! What did you do?"

"I tried to pick up a cop in the men's room in Pershing Square."

"You know that's the worst place for entrapment."

"I didn't think he was a cop. We were both at the urinals. Funny thing is, I really had to take a piss. He was standing there stroking himself and looking at me. He smiled and said, 'Hi,' so I said 'Hi.' I knew he wasn't turned on by my fat body, so I thought he must be a hustler."

"But weren't you afraid of him?"

"He was so cute, I thought it would be worth a chance, even if he had a knife. I said to him, 'How much?' He said, 'How much do you have?' I told him I had thirty dollars."

"He could have robbed you."

"I know, but his dick was so hard and beautiful, so I said I would give him the thirty dollars. He said I could give him a blow job. So we went in a stall. He dropped his pants, and his cock and balls were staring at me. I almost died. He said, 'You can drop your pants too and jerk off.' So I did. I was sucking him for about a minute when he says, 'You're under arrest.' He pulls out his badge and handcuffs me."

"Then what did he do?"

"He took me to the police station, and they booked me. They said I would have to stay overnight and go to court this morning. The judge set the bail at five thousand dollars."

"What did they charge you with?"

"Indecent exposure, soliciting a police officer, and other stuff. Will you call my father and tell him to wire you five thousand dollars? Then you can come bail me out."

"Should I tell him what happened?"

"Sure. He won't be surprised. His number is on a pad on the kitchen counter."

"Okay. What precinct are you in?"

"The fifth precinct. Try to hurry. I'm in a cell with a guy who is threatening to rape me."

"I'll be there as soon as I get the money."

After Philip did his good deed for the day and got his friend out of jail, he told Barry, "I think you're desperate because Mac left you."

Barry said, "You're probably right. That's why I'm going back to New York. I'm not a real photographer anyway."

Philip said, "But you love it. Why don't you take classes

and try to be an apprentice? Then you'll find out if you have any talent."

Philip thought that was what he himself was trying to do. It seemed so hopeless sometimes, but something drove him to keep trying.

There were incidents that offered hope and encouraged him to persist. Richard Chamberlain, after becoming a big star as Dr. Kildare, attempted to start a workshop for young actors at NBC. Philip auditioned and was chosen. He received an acceptance letter from Richard Chamberlain that he would treasure for the rest of his life. Unfortunately for the young actors, NBC backed out of the workshop.

Deborah, on the other hand, was more successful. While sitting in her agent's waiting room, she met another of his clients, who happened to be a famous leading man. Being married did not stop the actor from inviting her to lunch. Before long, she had a part in a big musical, and he visited her regularly, once she got rid of Mac.

Mac, having been thrown out of Deborah's apartment, asked Philip if he could sleep on his couch until he found another place. Barry had gone back to New York, so Mac's prospects were dim. Philip, feeling sorry for him, allowed Mac to sleep on his couch.

The first night, in the middle of the night, Mac crawled into bed with Philip. Philip awoke with a start. Mac tried to kiss him, but Philip resisted.

Mac said, "I could make you feel good."

Philip responded, "No, thanks. This isn't what I meant when I said you could stay here."

Exposing his huge erect penis, Mac said, "I know you want it."

Philip was tempted but said, "Barry is my friend. You know I wouldn't do anything to hurt him."

"Barry's not here. We both need someone. I always was attracted to you."

"Please don't make this difficult. Barry will come back one day," offered Philip, wondering what diseases Mac might have. He knew that Mac would have sex with him to have a place to live. Philip considered it for a moment, thinking it might help him to overcome his pain over losing John.

Mac grabbed Philip's hand and placed it on his hard penis. "Think of how this will feel going into your ass."

Philip knew that if he gave in to his desire for intimacy, Mac would be his downfall. He said, "I'm sorry. I can't. You'll have to leave tomorrow."

"You know I could rape you if I wanted. I'd show you what you're missing."

"I know you can. Please don't do that."

Mac slunk back to the sofa. He knew that he would be back hustling on Santa Monica Boulevard. It seemed that this was to be his life in the future. He had no education, and there were not many jobs he was qualified to perform. All he had to offer was his body.

Philip soon received a call that lifted his spirits—he had won the part in Roger Smith's play. He would be notified as soon as the team had all the financing and could begin rehearsals. He continued to work in the flower shop and to go to the neighborhood gay bar. But whenever he was attracted to someone, thoughts of John interfered with his forming a relationship.

His joy over being cast in a play was short-lived. The stage manager called to tell him the production had been canceled for lack of finances. Again he was plunged into depression.

John hadn't called since he got married. Philip began to wonder if he was not meant to be an actor.

Daily Variety became his bible. He scoured it for any news of movie castings. He read that Delbert Mann, the director who had won the Academy Award for *Marty,* was going to make a movie written by Tad Mosel, the acclaimed screenwriter. It would star Geraldine Page, Philip's favorite actress, and Glenn Ford, his dreamboat ever since he had seen Ford in *Gilda.* Somehow he managed to get through all the secretaries and speak with Delbert Mann, by mentioning the name of his acting teacher in New York, Eli Rill. Mann inquired about his friend Rill and said he would be pleased to meet a student of his. He graciously invited Philip to come to Paramount Studios to see him.

It was an ordeal to gain entrance to Paramount without a pass. The guard wanted every piece of identification Philip had in his wallet; then he called about ten people. Finally, he said that Philip had passed inspection and gave him directions to Mr. Mann's bungalow.

Intimidated by the huge sound stages that loomed before him, Philip made his way to the bungalow. It reminded him of a New England cottage. After a moment of panic over whether to ring the bell or knock on the door, he decided that a knock would be the lesser intrusion.

Mr. Mann opened the door. He was a tall man in his forties and looked like a kindly uncle. John relaxed immediately.

"Come in," said Mr. Mann.

"Thank you, sir," replied Philip.

Mr. Mann showed him into a spacious living room decorated in early American chintz. It was so homey that Philip didn't feel as if he were in an office. To top it off, there were tea and biscuits on the coffee table in front of the couch.

When Mr. Mann motioned for him to sit on the couch, Philip wondered if this would be one of the fabled "Hollywood casting couches." However, he had never heard any homosexual stories about Mr. Mann, who was married.

Mr. Mann said, "So you studied with Eli Rill."

Philip uttered, "Yes, sir."

"He's a good friend and the best acting teacher in New York."

Philip said, "I agree. He helped me a lot."

Mr. Mann continued, "There is a small part, the bellman in a hotel. It is a good scene, with Geraldine Page, who often stays at that hotel. She knows the bellman and asks him to help her rearrange the furniture to give it a homey look."

Philip practically screamed, "Oh, I love Geraldine Page." He didn't dare mention his affection for Glenn Ford. "I would love to audition for it."

Mr. Mann smiled. "If you studied with Eli, I'm sure you could do it. You don't have to audition for me."

Philip gushed, "Oh, thank you. That would be wonderful."

"I'll be in touch when we're ready to start production."

"I really appreciate this, sir."

Philip was elated. He couldn't believe that he would be in a movie with Geraldine Page and Glenn Ford. He would actually have a speaking part, with lines. It was a legitimate feature film. He couldn't help giving a smartass grin to the guard as he walked through the gates on his way out. Now his life had a purpose in Los Angeles. He prayed the movie would start soon.

His first call was to Carl and Sharon. They invited him to supper to celebrate. They couldn't know the depth of his appreciation for their friendship.

He still never felt like he was completely himself in Los

Angeles. In fact, he felt that the only time he had ever been able to be and reveal his complete self was when he had been with John in the army. Now, at this stage of his life, he was functioning: going to work, preparing simple meals, trying to make friends, and going out with acquaintances, but doing it all in a vacuum.

He went with a student from acting class to a party at Troy Donahue's house. He felt intimidated by Donahue, since he was a big star after making *A Summer Place* with Sandra Dee. However, Philip knew that it was important in Hollywood to make connections. Knowing that Henry Wilson was Donahue's agent and was known for his gay male clientele, Philip hoped he might get an introduction to Wilson.

Somehow Philip got involved in a conversation with Donahue himself about cashmere sweaters and Donahue's own collection of them.

"Want to come into my bedroom, and I'll show you my sweaters?" asked Donahue.

"Yes, I'd like to see them," answered Philip.

Donahue led him to the room and opened the doors of closets filling one wall. "I think I have every color. My friends know that I collect them and try to buy me a sweater wherever they are."

"I've never seen so many sweaters, especially cashmere, in one place outside of a store."

"Go ahead. Try one on. Pick out your favorite color."

"I'd be afraid I'd get it dirty."

"No, don't be silly. I insist."

Philip picked a turquoise sweater and put it on.

Donahue lay on his bed and said, "That's your color. It really looks good on you. Come here. I want to take the price tag off."

Tentatively, Philip approached the bed. He didn't know if Donahue was making a pass at him. Besides, he thought that a movie star wouldn't want anyone to see his penis, because people could gossip about it. Philip didn't know how this would permit them ever to have sex.

Donahue ripped off the tag and said, "It's yours."

"Oh, I couldn't take it."

"Why not? I want you to have it."

"It's too expensive."

"Okay, maybe after you get to know me better. Want to come to dinner next week?"

"Thanks, I'd like to."

But that never transpired. Philip was not surprised; when he gave Donahue his telephone number, he knew how difficult it would be for Donahue to find time for him.

Philip realized that he could not dwell on ideas of sex with anyone while in Hollywood. The process was foreign to him. So he devoted all his energy to acting class and to hoping that Delbert Mann's movie would start soon.

TWENTY

A Wrong Turn

A few days later, Philip awoke with excitement. He was going to meet Stanley, a friend from his acting class in New York who had recently moved to Los Angeles. Not only was Stanley a gay friend from home, but he was also very attractive. Philip had entertained ideas of going out with him when they were in New York, but their friendship had never progressed to that state.

Living in Los Angeles had been like drowning in an ocean, and Stanley appeared to be a life raft. Philip thought that he might finally be able to develop a relationship with a man without the shadow of John hanging over it.

When Stanley walked into Philip's apartment, he was a ray of sunshine. His pale blond hair streaked across Philip's vision, and his smiling green eyes pierced his heart. They hugged, and Philip kissed Stanley on the lips.

Stanley exclaimed, "Hey, I guess you are really happy to see me. It's so good to see you too. I don't know anyone here."

"Why did you decide to come to LA?"

"I was sick of the theater in New York. All I got were shitty parts in shitty off-Broadway plays."

"I know what you mean. That's what I have here. Shitty parts in off-off-Broadway plays. No movies."

"The first thing I need is a good lay. Do you know any black guys?"

"No, actually, I don't," answered Philip, trying to conceal his astonishment.

"I really got into black guys in New York. They do have big dicks. I need to get fucked."

"There's a gay bar nearby. We can go there after lunch if you want."

"Sure, let's go out to lunch first. My treat."

Philip realized that lunch was all he was going to get from Stanley. At least Stanley could be another friend, which Philip needed. Stanley had a car and drove Philip to the beach in Santa Monica. It was fun being with someone from his past. They talked about their classmates, some of whom were making it big, such as Barbra Streisand. But Helene, who had been the first person to record Barbra singing, had been murdered by her crazy boyfriend.

Philip had hoped that Stanley might share his apartment and help with the rent, since the owner of the building had finally made them all pay up and Philip was having difficulty paying his rent. Having a roommate would have helped. But Stanley had other ideas. His main goal was to have sex with as many black men as possible. A roommate would cramp his style.

So Philip had to move again, to an even cheaper apartment. He found one of those weird places in Los Angeles, a miniature house in the backyard of the modest home of an elderly couple. The tiny house had one room with a table and chair that abutted a single bed and, in the corner, a small refrigerator and a hot plate that together served as a kitchen. The little house actually had a separate bathroom with a toilet, sink, and shower too. Philip thought, *What more does one need?*

Carl and Sharon worried about Philip being lonely and gave him a kitten. Philip had never had a cat before. He prepared a little bed for it on the floor next to his own bed and made a toy for it by tying a long string to a small stuffed ball and fastening the string to the counter. The kitten loved to play with it.

Philip took the kitten everywhere. Even when Carl picked him up to go for a drive, Philip took the kitten. It was a new relationship for both Philip and the kitten, which loved to sit on Philip's head and bury itself in the curls and waves of his hair. The kitten also liked to sleep in Philip's bed and cuddle up next to his hair while Philip was trying to sleep. Philip didn't particularly like this and usually pushed the kitten aside and went back to sleep. However, one morning when he was especially on edge, the kitten jumped on him, and Philip reacted more violently. He sprang out of bed, grabbed the kitten, and threw it out into the yard. Then he went back to sleep.

When he awoke, he went into a panic over the kitten. He ran into the yard, calling, "Kitten! Kitten!" He had never given it a name. He was upset that he had sent the poor defenseless animal out to fend for itself. Ashamed and crestfallen, he returned to his little house, where he found the kitten crouched beside the step. Philip lavished kisses upon his found friend. Realizing he could not take care of the kitten, he returned it to Carl.

He knew he had to find friends to fill the void. A man named Bill, who looked like a cheap version of Errol Flynn, lived across the street—or rather inhabited a cave-like dwelling in the garage across the street. Philip was drawn to his tawdry appearance. He looked like he would have sex with anyone. Philip gazed across the street at him and knew that he must be an actor.

"Hi!" shouted Philip.

"Hi, yourself," laughed Bill. "Come over."

"I just moved in."

"You still look fresh. Wait awhile. You'll look like the rest of us."

"What do you mean?" Philip asked.

"You'll get that mean and hungry look."

"You don't look that way."

"Come on. I know I do. I also know I've got what you want. Come into my lair."

Philip followed him into the garage. It was claustrophobic, with a low ceiling. There was a bed, but no chairs, so Philip had to sit on the bed. Bill stood in front of him and unzipped his pants. He pulled out his semierect penis and placed it on Philip's lips. Without saying a word, Philip opened his mouth and sucked him in. Bill moaned, encouraging Philip to go faster. Philip's pleasure was in knowing that he was giving another human being pleasure. Bill pushed him back onto the bed and climbed on top of him. He pulled Philip's pants off and raised his legs over his shoulders. He pushed his penis into Philip's rectum. Philip grimaced with pain from the sudden intrusion. After a few strokes, he became aroused and clenched Bill's penis with his anal muscles. He didn't want to let go, but Bill had other ideas. He furiously pumped until he came, which triggered Philip's ejaculation.

"I've never come so fast," gasped Philip.

"Stick with me, kid, and I'll make you see stars. Then it won't matter if we don't become stars."

"How did you know I was an actor?"

"What else would you be doing here?"

"You're right. What else could I do at this point?"

"What do you mean?"

"I'm having sex with a stranger. I can't get a job acting. I might as well have a good time."

"You can't tell anyone about this," Bill said. "I'm known as a ladies' man. You have to have an image here."

"I know. Love doesn't matter, does it?"

"I don't have time for love. I have to become a star, have to be famous just to be normal. I never had anything growing up. Now I'm going to have everything. I'll get it one way or another. Isn't that what you want?"

Philip said, "I don't know anymore. I got love and art all mixed up. Now I don't have either one."

"You're too serious. No one in Hollywood wants to be serious or be with anyone who is serious."

"I can't help it. That's the way I am."

"Then act the part. Act being a movie star."

"Will you show me?"

"We can have sex, but don't get any idea of a relationship."

"Okay. Whatever you say."

"I'll take you to a party in a couple of hours."

All Philip knew about the party was that those attending it would be people in the business. One of Bill's friends had a car that they piled into. Philip was briefly introduced as a young actor, and he and Bill sat on the laps of three men in the back seat. As the car swerved on the narrow roads, the man whose lap Philip sat on grabbed Philip's penis. It started to harden, as did the man's penis beneath Philip. He was afraid to say anything as the young man squeezed his penis. When they arrived at the house, the young man jumped out of the car and winked at Philip. "See you inside," he said with a grin.

A swimming pool full of naked men greeted them. Sunbeams bounced off the turquoise water onto suntanned bodies, while peals of laughter attacked Philip. He was introduced to the host, a famous leading man whom all the ladies drooled over. Philip thought about his aunt Helen back home, who would never believe that this movie star was gay, even if he had sex with a man right in front of her. He was the epitome of masculinity.

When the movie star invited him up to his bedroom, Philip could not resist. This was a dream come true. Philip expected the star to mount him the way he had the many stallions he had ridden in the movies.

Philip sat on the bed and watched, mesmerized, as the star removed his clothes. When he was finished, he told Philip to strip. As Philip got up from the bed, the star lay down on the bed—facedown. Once more, Philip was stunned. He couldn't believe that the star wanted to be penetrated. This was not Philip's favorite position. He was quick to ask for a condom.

"I always get urinary tract infections, sir," mumbled Philip.

"No shit. There's some in the night table. Come here first and let me suck you."

"Yes, sir." Philip walked to the night table and grabbed a fistful of condoms and then walked to the side of the bed.

The star said, "You have a beautiful cock. Come closer." He devoured Philip's erection.

"Oh," gasped Philip.

"Now stick it in me while it's hard."

Philip rode the famous actor. Every scene that he had fantasized about was now a reality. Philip was so overcome with fantasy, emotion, and physical sensations that he wasn't aware who was fucking whom. After he finished, Philip was struck by the fact that he had not once thought of John. He realized that intense physical sensation could block out his mental longing for him. However, he was dumbfounded when he realized that he was thinking about John right now.

The star said, "You're very good. You made me come. Not everyone can do that."

"Thank you, sir."

"I'll tell Henry about you. Go to see him Monday morning."

Philip knew he meant Henry Wilson, his agent. Philip was so appreciative that he gave him a hug and kiss.

⌗

On Monday morning, he called Henry Wilson's office. There was an appointment scheduled for him at eleven o'clock.

As Philip walked up Sunset Boulevard at ten in the morning, he thought it should be called Sunrise Boulevard, with its gleaming white buildings and blinding light. Although he knew he was not the "type" that Mr. Wilson liked, he hoped the agent would take some interest in him upon the star's recommendation.

That did not turn out to be the case at all. The only interest Mr. Wilson showed was when Philip told him about the upcoming movie with Delbert Mann. Wilson said that he would call the studio to find out when Mann's movie would begin and that he would be happy to negotiate for Philip. Of course, he would take his usual commission. Philip felt this would be worth it to get his foot in the door.

As time passed and there was no word from either Wilson or Mann, Philip began to doubt anything would happen before his money ran out. His landlords allowed him to paint their living room in lieu of rent. He appreciated his aunt Helen for having taught him how to paint and the many hours they had spent painting at Philip's grandparents' house.

Then his money finally ran out. He didn't want to ask his parents for any more, so he sadly decided he had to go home.

So many wonderful experiences had been tinged with sadness. He reviewed his life and tried to make sense of it. He thought about one of his best experiences in the army, with Jim. This was one completely untouched by sadness. He and Jim had parted in a loving way. He had heard that Jim had knocked up a German girl and had had to marry her. In the midst of his current sadness in LA, Philip wanted to see Jim one last time. He contacted the army with Jim's address in Schwäbisch Gmünd and learned that Jim had reenlisted and was working in the CO's office in Oklahoma City. Philip called him.

"Hello, may I speak with Jim?" Philip asked the person who answered the phone.

"Just a minute," replied a gruff voice.

"Hello," said Jim.

"Hi, Jim?" Philip said excitedly.

"Who is this?" said Jim, obviously annoyed.

"It's me, Philip."

"How did you get this number?"

"I tracked you down from our last assignment in Germany."

"Where are you?"

"I'm in Los Angeles, but things haven't worked out. I'm going back to New York and could stop in Oklahoma City to see you."

"I don't think that's a good idea."

"Oh, okay. I'm sorry."

Philip was crushed. He didn't know if Jim was happily married or not. However, he had thought that they could have their long-delayed date in a hotel, not in Germany but in Oklahoma City. They could have had a moment of joy and pleasure. Since this was not going to happen, he immediately called American Airlines to book the next direct flight to New York City.

Shortly after this, the phone rang.

"Hello," said a despondent Philip.

"Hi, it's Jim," said a cheerful Jim.

"Yes?"

"I couldn't talk before. My sergeant was right next to me. Will you come to Oklahoma? I know a hotel you can stay at."

"Too late. I already booked my flight to New York."

"I really want to see you. I can stay overnight with you in the hotel."

"What will you tell your wife?"

"I'll tell her that I have guard duty. Sometimes I have to stay in the office overnight."

"What do you want to do?"

"Everything that we couldn't do in Schwäbisch Gmünd."

"I would have liked that too. But now it's too late."

"Can't you change your flight?"

"I don't want to. Goodbye."

TWENTY-ONE

Parting of the Clouds

As the plane cut through the clouds to make its land-ing at Idlewild Airport in New York, a patch of blue sky washed over Philip. He felt a weight lifting from his shoulders. He was free. But what would he do now with his leftover life?

His first stop was at the Actors' Equity Association office to look for a job. Companies posted notices at the Equity office when they wanted someone who could memorize and learn their business quickly.

Philip soon found a job as a research assistant in a law firm on Wall Street. It paid enough for him to rent a basement apartment on Central Park West for eight-five dollars per month, in a town house shaped like a castle with a turret. The apartment windows were flush with the sidewalk. Philip found it fascinating to watch shoes and legs pass by without the pedestrians' awareness.

The wide marble steps leading to the front door reminded him of Europe. Philip imagined that one day he would come home to find John sitting on the steps. He made sure that he was correctly listed in the phone book so that John would be able to find him. Every day, he looked at the empty steps and never gave up hope that John would follow him. He could never accept the fact that he would not see John again.

Working at the law firm, he was allowed to take time off for auditions. Other actors worked there too, so Philip found the atmosphere to be pleasant and convivial.

Then, on the afternoon of November 22, 1963, the boss made an announcement. He said, "You can all go home. President Kennedy has been assassinated."

Philip felt a punch to his stomach. "It can't be true."

"I'm afraid it is."

He remembered his sadness when Marilyn Monroe had died; President Kennedy had been shot just a little over a year after Marilyn's death.

Philip walked to the subway with a few coworkers. The streets were silent, with no horns blaring. The train was deathly quiet. He heard some sniffles, but that was all. There was no conversation or communication among the riders. It was the only time he had witnessed this phenomenon. He thought of the phrase "father of his country." Had that been George Washington? Now he realized that Kennedy had been *his* father of the country. He felt lost as he walked home from the subway. He had no idea what he would do next.

Philip's grief was compounded later that same day when he learned that shooting had been completed for *Dear Heart*, the Delbert Mann film he should have been in. Again he felt lost, with something like a sense of betrayal nagging at his heart. He quit his job and went to stay with his family in upstate New York, planning to spend Christmas and New Year's Day with them.

Upon his return to New York some months later, he saw a casting call for German-speaking American actors to join

West Berlin's Schiller Theater, which would open the new State Theater in Lincoln Center on November 24, 1964. Philip was cast as a Spanish nobleman in *Don Carlos*, which ran for a couple of weeks, and as a prisoner in *The Captain of Köpenick*, which ran for a few more weeks.

Being in the plays at Lincoln Center gave him an Equity contract, which meant that he was now eligible to join the union. However, after his stint at Lincoln Center, his acting career proceeded downward to small off-Broadway theaters.

Philip needed something more meaningful in his life, so he applied for the civil service test to become a caseworker for the welfare department. He got the job, which paid him a hundred dollars a week to work in Harlem.

Through a friend at work, he received an invitation to spend the weekend at Fire Island, the gay paradise. Philip's friend was married but had affairs with men. Philip met Keith, another caseworker in Harlem, at that weekend retreat. Keith was getting a divorce. Philip asked Keith to take a walk on the beach at dusk. The ocean swirled with various colors as they walked side by side on the white sand.

Philip asked, "How do you like working for the welfare department?"

"It's okay, but I really want to get a PhD in sociology," replied Keith.

"Why sociology?"

"I want to study human behavior. I'm curious about what motivates someone to act in a particular way. I love conducting experiments."

"It seems like our lives are experiments."

"I think that's true. When I got married, I thought Mary was the only person in the world for me. Then one night we were walking in the village, past the theater where *The*

Fantasticks was playing. The show was over, and the actors were coming out. We stopped to look at them, and I caught one of the actors staring at me. I smiled. He came over and kissed me—on the lips, long and passionate, in front of everyone. I knew in that moment that I wanted to have sex with him. My wife made a joke of it, and we all laughed. The next night, I went to see the show—alone. I went backstage and asked him to go for a drink. The actor said, 'Why don't you come to my place for that drink?' I told him I would like that. We went to his walk-up apartment in Hell's Kitchen. As soon as we closed the door, he tore off my clothes. I grabbed him and kissed him. We made love more intensely than I ever had with a woman. When it was over, he told me it had been great, but he had a boyfriend. I was dumbstruck and quickly left. I couldn't have him, but I knew that I wanted a man. So I told my wife, and we agreed to get a divorce."

Philip looked at Keith with a desire he had not felt in a long time.

"Say something," implored Keith.

Philip was aware of the roar of the ocean and the waves coming to shore. His heart was filled by them. He felt the ocean pushing him toward Keith. He uttered, "I don't know what to say."

"You look like you're going to kiss me."

"I want to."

"Not here. Come to my apartment when we get back to the city tomorrow."

"I'll be there."

Philip found it hard to believe that Keith did not just want sex on this island of sun, sand, and sex. He would have given that pleasure to Keith, since he had become accustomed to having sex with strangers. Was it possible that Keith was looking for a relationship?

The next night, they talked for hours about Sartre. They both subscribed to his philosophy of being alone in this world. They wanted to give each other a moment of comfort but ultimately believed that they had come into the world alone and would leave it alone. As they sat by the fireplace in Keith's apartment, the warm and intellectual atmosphere reminded Philip of college. By the time Philip went to bed with Keith, he was ready to bare his soul. He felt free to give his body and—yes—his love to him.

Philip was falling in love with Keith. He thought about him all the time. He became excited whenever Keith was coming to his apartment. They would have dinner and then go to bed. Philip loved every part of Keith's body. So when Keith said, "I think we have to have anal intercourse to be true homosexuals," Philip was ready. He had bought condoms in anticipation of this moment. Keith was first to penetrate Philip. Then he asked Philip to do the same to him.

Feeling a bond, Philip said, "I'm going to put a gold chain on you and walk you through the park." They both laughed and went out to walk in Central Park, but at the time, Philip did not realize the effect his remark had had on Keith.

Later on, Keith made it clear that he did not want a monogamous relationship. He wanted to experiment with other men. Philip, on the other hand, wanted no other man. He was completely satisfied with Keith's mind and body. But Keith was frightened off by Philip's possessiveness, and before long he had moved on to a relationship with another man named Philip.

Desperate to find a part in a play, Philip went to every audition possible. He finally was cast in a play written by Andy

Warhol's screenwriter. It would have a lavish off-Broadway opening, with Warhol attending. Hoping to be written up in one of the gossip columns, Philip adopted the stage name Warhol Greco, claiming he liked the sound of the name *Warhol*. He started getting publicity to the point that one of the actors, out of jealousy, started a fight with him onstage.

During rehearsals he was invited to Andy Warhol's studio, The Factory. Andy looked very pale. He had white skin and had bleached his hair white, so he appeared ghostlike but not frightening. He was soft-spoken to the point that some people called him namby-pamby. He made movies that were ambiguous so that people could project their own confusion onto them. But behind this facade was a brilliant mind that could predict the next trend in society. Philip was intrigued by his mind. Andy perceived this and could relax when he was with Philip, knowing that Philip didn't want anything from him.

Andy had just become famous for painting *Campbell's Soup Cans*. Various publications, including *Time* magazine, made fools of themselves trying to give the painting some deep meaning. Andy told Philip he had made the painting because his mother often gave him Campbell soup when he was a child.

Andy added to his mystique by having his studio in a warehouse where visitors had to take a freight elevator to reach it. When Philip went there for the first time, Maria Callas's voice boomed through the airshaft as he ascended to the studio. Then Philip was overpowered by the glare of the tinfoil that covered the ceiling and the walls in the studio. Andy had completely captivated him by tacking up Philip's headshot on his bulletin board, next to those of Mick Jagger and Rudolph Nureyev.

One Sunday Andy invited Philip to come to his town house

to pick him up and walk to The Factory. Philip was astonished to see that Andy lived in a dilapidated town house on Lexington Avenue, in a posh Upper East Side location. They had to climb over wooden beams to get to the living room. Andy explained that the beams were part of a reconstruction project. One reason he had bought the building was that there was an apartment on the top floor that he thought would make a comfortable space for his mother.

The only place to sit was a dusty love seat, so they had to sit close to each other. Andy said he was going to give Philip a name, as he had with "Ultra Violet" and others. He said he would call him "Rose" because he smelled like one.

Philip exclaimed, "Oh, you can't. I'm a legitimate actor!"—unlike the people who usually appeared in Andy's films, Philip thought.

Andy said, "But I love the way you smell."

Philip explained, "It's Givenchy aftershave. I'll buy you a bottle. We can get it at Bloomingdale's."

Andy nodded. "Yes, I would like that."

Philip was not worried that Andy would make a pass because he knew that Andy was not aggressive. He also knew that he could talk his way out of this line of conversation. Philip said, "My part in the play is very complicated. Your writer did a good job of giving the character such a wide range. I have to go from an adult to a child throwing a temper tantrum." Philip continued to talk about his part until Andy dozed off.

When Andy woke up, he said, "I know another part that you would be good for. Do you know Tennessee Williams's short story 'Desire and the Black Masseur'?"

Philip said, "Yes. I can identify with the loneliness of the character, but I'm too young."

"We can change his age."

"Also, I've seen how you shoot movies with no special effects. The masseur would really have to break my bones."

Andy laughed and said, "Let's walk to The Factory. That's the only exercise I get."

"Great. It's a beautiful sunny day."

⁛

When the play opened, Andy kept his promise and attended. The press came to see Andy, not the play itself. All the publicity convinced an agent to see the show too, and when he met Philip, he told Philip he could send him on an interview. Andy also introduced Philip to a producer who wanted to make a film of "Desire and the Black Masseur"; Andy wanted Philip to play the part they had discussed. However, Paramount owned the rights to the short story and would not release them, even though the studio would never make the movie.

Soon the agent sent Philip to see the director Frank Perry, who had directed *David and Lisa*. Philip had loved that movie and was happy to meet him.

Mr. Perry said, "Are you Italian?"

Philip truthfully said, "Yes."

"Good. I'm planning a movie with Loren and Mastroianni in Rome. I need an American who speaks Italian. Do you?"

Philip untruthfully said, "Yes, sure, my whole family is Italian."

"I need someone I can speak to in English, so he will understand the nuances. I don't speak Italian. But the actor also has to speak some lines in Italian."

"I would give anything to work with Loren and Mastroianni," Philip said.

Mr. Perry said, "As soon as production is ready, I'll have you read the part."

Philip immediately enrolled in an Italian class at New York University. He did know a lot of vocabulary from his family but had no idea about grammar. He appreciated his ancestors' language for the first time.

While Philip tried to wait patiently, Mr. Perry called to say that they couldn't raise the money in Italy and the movie had been canceled. Philip was determined to go back to Rome anyway. He was in awe of the Italian directors: Fellini, Antonioni, De Sica, Visconti, and Pasolini. He had to get back to Rome.

After all, he had thrown a coin in the Trevi Fountain during his army days, when he had visited Rome with John, to assure his return. He asked every actor he knew for contacts in Rome and booked his flight.

TWENTY-TWO

Arrival in Act Two of Life

When Philip arrived in Rome in 1969, the city ap-peared completely different to him than it had in 1960, when he had been there with John. He was pleased. It was almost as if he were traveling to Rome for the first time. This time his intent was different. He was not on vacation with John but was in Rome to get work in the cinema. Working at Cinecita, the main studio, was his goal, not seeing the Colosseum.

It was July 20, 1969, and Philip wanted to be sure to watch the first man land on the moon—on the very same day that he had landed in Rome. His friend Dutch, an American who had played Tevye in *Fiddler on the Roof,* had given him the name of an American actress, Jane, who was living in Rome. Philip phoned her and asked, "Would you like to watch the moon landing?"

"Yes, but we don't have a TV in my pensione."

"I think we should be able to see it at the American embassy."

"That's a good idea," replied Jane.

Philip suggested, "Let's meet at the embassy on the Veneto."

After a warm greeting, they tried to go into the American embassy. A guard informed them that it was closed: "No entrata."

Now Philip really knew he was back in Italy. They went across the street to the Excelsior Hotel and found a television in the lobby. A few people were watching the static. Unfortunately, that was all they could see. Philip hoped his vision would be clearer as he tried to break into Italian cinema.

Dutch had also told him about a pensione near the Via Veneto, so he had made a reservation there. When he arrived, he discovered it was just a large apartment that an old Italian woman who was called "Mama" had inherited. She rented rooms, but there were no hotel amenities. Not only that, but she had not been expecting Philip until the next night. She ranted and raved, as Italians were wont to do.

Philip remembered this aspect of Italy, and he remained calm. Finally, he asked, "Do you have a cot?"

She did. They set it up in the dining room, and the problem was solved.

Philip was happy to find that *The Rome Daily American* was still being published. He read that a movie—a coproduction of Italy, America, and Germany, starring Hugh Hefner's current girlfriend—was being shot locally, and a well-known actor in Italy was shooting a scene at the Hilton hotel. Philip went to the hotel and was able to speak with the German director. After a few preliminary questions about Philip's acting background in New York, the director was sufficiently impressed to give him a small but important part. He even gave him the name of an agent who would negotiate his contract.

So a few weeks after arriving in Rome, Philip had a

legitimate contract for a role in a big feature film. He quickly discovered that this was no guarantee of an enjoyable artistic experience. The first problem was getting his agent to send him the script, since he wanted to memorize his part: Philip was to play the owner of a beautiful hotel by the sea whose good friends were spending their honeymoon at the hotel, presumably as a gift from the groom's father. In the script the father and son have an argument, and Philip's character receives a telegram from the groom's father stating that he will no longer pay the hotel bill. He shows his friend the telegram, and when the friend confesses that he knew his father wouldn't pay and he himself has no money and can't pay, Philip's character expresses his disappointment, which escalates into anger.

By the time Philip arrived on the set, he had already memorized his lines. The lead American actor asked him if he would like to rehearse the scene. Philip was pleased, not having expected this from a Hollywood movie star, but it turned out that the actor had been given the wrong script and had to learn new lines. The director called them to the set, not knowing whether they had rehearsed and not caring. He gave a few blocking directions and then started to shoot.

The thought that his character's good friend would lie to him affected Philip deeply. He got worked up emotionally until he hit a peak of anger. The director told Philip that he wanted him to pause before the last line and then say it calmly. He didn't explain why he wanted this, but he immediately called for a retake of the shot. Philip had to concentrate on how he handled the telegram from his friend's father to make sure the master shot coincided with the close-up. Once again, he got caught up in emotion and hit the peak at the end of his speech.

The German director screamed and insulted Philip. *Most likely, he is used to insulting German actors*, Philip thought, but he was stunned.

The lead actor with whom he had the scene didn't say a word. However, one of the other actors pulled Philip aside. He was Jose Luis de Vilallonga, who had been Audrey Hepburn's Brazilian love interest in *Breakfast at Tiffany's*. Vilallonga said, "Don't listen to him. You are doing a great job in the scene. It doesn't make sense to do what he asks."

Philip replied, "Once I get so emotional, I just can't turn it off."

"He should be glad you have memorized all the lines in that scene. It is very long. I never memorize that many lines for one take."

Philip said, "I had to pester my agent to get the script. I learned in New York to memorize everything before you get to the set. They even gave the wrong scene to the other actor."

Vilallonga said, "Keep doing what you're doing. You are right."

"Thank you. I appreciate that because this is my first movie in Rome."

They finished the scene, with the director still screaming. Philip reminded him that he was supposed to film another scene, in which Philip's character was to go out in a small boat to meet a yacht and bring his friends to his hotel.

The director had completely overlooked this scene. He was embarrassed and said, "*Jawohl*, we shoot it tomorrow."

Philip quietly said, "You have to pay me for another day, according to my contract."

The director fumed, "I'll pay for your room and food at the hotel, but no salary."

Philip smiled. "No, thank you. I'm going home." His real

reason for leaving was that he did not trust the director not to drown him. He gladly would have worked for nothing if he could have roomed with the leading actor, who had a propensity for taking off all his clothes to cool off in his bikini underwear between scenes.

Philip made enough money to move into a different pensione, on the Via del Babuino, near Piazza di Spagna. It was a modest and clean hotel with small rooms and friendly staff. Sarah Churchill, daughter of Sir Winston Churchill, often stayed there. She loved the ambience and the young Italian manager, who was a closeted gay man. This pensione was one of the few places a man could bring another man to his room for sex. And Fellini lived on the street behind the pensione, the Via Margutta. Philip hoped that he might run into the great director.

One of Philip's friends in New York had given him the name of an American opera singer staying in Rome. She kindly invited him to attend a concert in her apartment. Philip was overjoyed to meet Americans living in Rome. One of them, Robert, would later become his roommate. Another one who would become a close friend was Roloff Beny, a Canadian photographer who was drawn to Philip and invited him to his penthouse on Lungotevere Ripa in Trasteveri.

Philip would meet everyone who was anyone in Rome at Roloff's salon on Sundays. Peggy Guggenheim was one of those people. She sat on the settee, holding court, in the room Roloff called the Elephant Ballroom, which was wall-papered with life-size photographs he had taken of elephants in Africa.

A drunken Irish poet from Boston confronted Peggy: "What have you ever done to help anyone with all your money? I'm an artist. I give something to the world. What do you give? You only take. You shouldn't be allowed to be on this earth, you cunt."

Peggy looked him in the eye during his speech. After he finished, she turned to her companion on the settee and continued her conversation. She didn't miss a beat.

Gore Vidal was a friend of Roloff and was writing the epilogue for Roloff's book *Roloff Beny in Italy*. One evening Philip went to Roloff's apartment for dinner, and Vidal came after dinner to discuss the book. He had to speak first, like the Queen of England. Philip left the room without saying a word to him. After thirty minutes, Vidal came into the living room to fetch Philip. He began to regale them with stories of the famous people he knew. He told them that he had goosed Hugh Hefner in the men's room while standing next to him at the urinals. He said that Hef had gone ballistic—hardly the reaction that you would expect from someone so free with sex.

Philip had distant relatives living in Rome, and they invited Philip to a party in their apartment. There he met their friend Paolo, who was slim and had long blond hair, gray eyes, and a swagger similar to the boy in the film *Death in Venice*. Paolo wanted to be an actor. Although he had no contacts in the world of cinema, at the age of twenty-four he had the advantage of youth. Philip wanted him to succeed and hoped he could help him, so he invited him to his thirty-third birthday party. Paolo was thrilled to attend a party with Americans. Before this, he had seen them only in the movies.

In the excitement on the night of the party, Philip spilled a drink on Paolo's pants. He took him into the bathroom and tried to spot-clean them with soap and water. The spots were on Paolo's crotch, and under the guise of cleaning them, Philip was feeling his penis. When Paolo started to get hard, Philip said, "I have to go to a casting call tomorrow. Do you want to come with me?"

Paolo replied, "Yes. I'll pick you up. What time?"

Having been told that Paolo went to clubs with his friends every night, Philip said, "I'll come to your apartment at ten in the morning and wake you up."

The next morning, promptly at ten, Philip rang Paolo's bell.

A groggy Paolo opened the door. "I just have to rest for half an hour. Okay?"

Philip accompanied him to his bedroom and lay beside him on the bed. They had sex, and Philip basked in the afterglow of this beautiful creature having had sex with him. When Paolo was ready to go, he told Philip not to tell anyone what they had done. He was a stud around women.

Because Philip lived within walking distance of Paolo's apartment, this morning ritual happened quite often from then on. At last Philip was satisfied sexually. He didn't expect more.

Before leaving New York, Philip had read an article in the *New York Times* about American actors living in Rome. Carroll Baker had been featured since she represented the typical American beauty. Roloff had rented one of his apartments to Carroll when she first arrived in Rome, so Philip had previously asked to be introduced to her. Roloff's personality was similar to Andy Warhol's—involving a lot of procrastination. Finally, Roloff gave Philip Carroll's phone number and told him to call her.

After much hesitation, Philip finally called her. He said, "Hi. I'm a friend of Roloff's. I'm an actor from New York."

Carroll said, "How is New York? I miss it."

"It's still wild. Something always going on. I read the article about you in the *New York Times*."

Carroll responded, "It was a nice article."

Philip said, "I wonder if we could meet sometime."

Carroll groaned, "I get up when it's dark, and I come home when it's dark, so if you want to see me, you better come to the studio."

Philip was thrilled about going to see her at the studio. "Oh, I would love to."

"Okay, it's the De Paolis studio. I'll leave your name at the gate tomorrow."

"Thanks. I look forward to meeting you."

Philip walked into his first movie studio in Rome. He was anxious, not knowing how to get around or even what picture Carroll was making. He finally found the sound stage and walked in on her shower scene with Jean Sorel, the French actor. He tried not to look at their naked bodies, especially that of Sorel, who was the sexiest guy he had ever seen.

After a couple of takes, Carroll grabbed a white terrycloth robe and rushed over to meet Philip. She reminded him of Marilyn Monroe in *The Seven Year Itch*. Shivering, Carroll said, "Would you be a dear and get me a cup of hot coffee?"

"Yes, sure," Philip managed to say.

As Carroll drank her coffee, they talked about things they had in common, such as their birthdays in May, making them both Geminis. It was one of those rare moments when you met a stranger and felt as if you had known the person all your life. An everlasting bond was formed.

One night as they sat in Piazza Navona, across from Bernini's fountain, Carroll asked Philip if he could type.

"Can I type? Three courses and ninety words per minute," he laughed. He told her about his army experience.

"I can get you a job as my personal secretary on the film I'm going to do in London."

"London? That is fantastic. I was there for ten hours when I was in the army on my way to Germany. I loved London. I was in uniform, and two gay boys picked me up in Piccadilly Circus. They showed me the town, but unfortunately, I couldn't stay the night. I had to get back to the ship in Southampton by midnight."

"Maybe you'll find those gay boys when we go to London," laughed Carroll.

They arrived to great fanfare in London. The director was pleased to have Philip looking after Carroll, even though he had already assigned her a limousine and a chauffeur. He also asked Philip to read for a small part, and Philip got it. When they began shooting, Philip was immediately accepted by the cast and crew because he was a friend of the star. He took care of Carroll's every need, so she was free to concentrate on her part. He always had dinner with her so that she would not be alone.

At the request of an actor friend in New York, Philip called Hardy Amies, who was world-renowned for his clothing for Queen Elizabeth II. The elegance of a true English gentleman was audible in Mr. Amies's voice on the phone. He was happy to hear from a friend of his good friend in New York, and he graciously invited Philip to a "men's dinner" at his house that same night. When Philip told Carroll, she told him to go and said she would have dinner in her room. Philip looked forward to this new adventure into English society.

Philip was pleased with himself for having learned how to travel by the London Underground. He took it to the High Street Kensington tube station. From there it was a short walk to Eldon Road and Mr. Amies's mansion. Philip was greeted and waited on by several stewards before he was presented to the drawing room of guests and Mr. Amies and his partner Ken Fleetwood. Philip was the only American, making him the center of attention. Although all eyes were on him, he himself was looking into the eyes of Sir Nigel, another guest. He felt a sharp tingle rising from his toes.

Sir Nigel moved to Philip's side before any other handsome gentleman in the group might do so. "I love Americans," pronounced Sir Nigel.

"Why?" inquired Philip sincerely.

"You are so direct. It is almost naive, in a good way."

"But you Englishmen are more charming," continued Philip.

"It's just an act. Manners cover a lot of rubbish."

"We Americans find it elegant."

"Then I hope you will find me elegant enough to allow me to take you home after dinner. I hope you don't think I'm too forward, but I want to get my bid in before the others sweep down on you. You are so handsome."

"That is what I mean. No matter what you say, as long as you have an English accent, it sounds poetic. I do think you are so handsome also, and I would like you to take me home."

"Then it's settled. I'll let you circulate, but don't forget about me."

"Okay," laughed Philip. "How could I?"

Mr. Amies showed Philip around the house, which was filled with antiques and mementos from the royal family. The carved wood-paneled walls and damask-covered Victorian sofas conveyed the grandeur of Great Britain.

Amies said, "I saw the way Nigel looked at you. That's the first time in a very long time that I have seen that look. He is a wonderful man. He has had some disastrous relationships in the past, but now he is forty and has matured. He would love to have a partner, so if you are interested in him, please give him a chance. I wouldn't encourage you with some of the other guests. They are my friends, but they are pretentious. Nigel is special."

Philip, a bit shaken, said, "I do like him. But I'm not going to be in London much longer. I'm just working on this movie with Carroll Baker, and then we go back to Rome."

Amies replied, "Please keep an open mind. Anything is possible."

The dinner was fun. Even the bitchy queens were clever and amusing. Every once in a while, Philip looked across the table at Nigel. He always caught Nigel staring at him. Philip involuntarily smiled back. He thought, *I must be mad to think of any type of relationship with Nigel except sex.* After dinner, they played charades, and the group good-naturedly teased Philip about his American accent.

When it was time to leave, Nigel brought Philip's coat to him. He was the perfect gentleman. As they exited Amies's house, a black Rolls-Royce pulled up. The chauffer got out and opened the door.

"Oh, I can't," stuttered Philip.

"What's the matter? Don't you like the car?" Nigel asked.

"I took the Underground here. I don't have a limousine," Philip answered.

"Please come to my house. We'll take the tube if you want. I don't want to do anything you don't want to do."

"I'm just not used to this."

"You can just ignore all of this. It means nothing to me. I just want to be with you."

"Okay. Let's take the car to your house."

When they arrived at Nigel's house in Mayfair, Philip was overwhelmed. He tried to be comfortable with all the luxury because Nigel seemed so sincere. Servants greeted them and asked if they wanted anything.

Philip told Nigel he was tired, and they went upstairs to Nigel's bedroom, where a servant brought an overnight kit to Philip. Nigel brought him a pair of silk pajamas.

When they got into bed, Nigel said, "I just want to hold you and kiss you. I don't want to have sex because I don't want this to be a one-night stand. I want to get to know you. I want to take you to dinner tomorrow."

"You surprise me," exclaimed Philip. "I don't know what you want. I thought we would just have sex."

"There is something about you that I like very much. I want you to give us a chance to see what develops."

"Okay."

Nigel gently kissed Philip and held him until he fell asleep. The next morning, Philip had to return to his hotel to pick up Carroll to go to the set. He told her that Nigel wanted to take them to dinner that evening. Carroll was pleased to go with them, as long as she could get home early because she had an early call on the set the next day.

Nigel picked them up in his Rolls-Royce. This time he drove, hoping to put Philip at ease. He took them to the Garrick Club, an actors' haven, for dinner. They were thrilled to be in the midst of English theater history. The sumptuous dining room, lit by chandeliers, was warm and inviting. Nigel had a special table prepared with white orchids to honor Carroll. He had a wicked sense of humor that reminded both Philip and Carroll of Oscar Wilde. Philip was surprised to see this side of Nigel. He was intrigued and puzzled at the same time.

After dinner Nigel drove them back to their hotel. Carroll quickly said her goodbyes and disappeared inside the building. Once they were alone in the car, Nigel kissed Philip. When Philip melted into his arms, Nigel asked if he could stay the night. Philip was happy that their first sexual experience would be in his own hotel room and not in Nigel's mansion. He wanted to be sure Nigel realized that Philip wanted him and not his money or stature.

Inside Philip's room, Nigel said, "You don't know how I have longed for this."

Philip lovingly said, "I've been thinking about this also. I want you, and I want you to want me."

"Oh, I do. Please let me make love to you and show you how I feel."

They quickly shed their clothes and rolled onto the plush comforter, adding to their sensual pleasure. Nigel lay on top of Philip and kissed him from his eyelids to his toes. He then moved upward to Philip's erect penis and took it in his mouth. The way he made love to Philip's penis assured Philip of Nigel's desire for him. He felt that Nigel enjoyed every line and curve of his penis.

Nigel murmured, "I love you. I love you. Please take me into your body." His erection pressed into Philip's penis. He carefully took Philip's legs and placed them on his shoulders, exposing his anus.

Philip excitedly took Nigel's penis and inserted it into his rectum. He tingled at the movement of Nigel's penis inside him. Although it was huge, Philip was so relaxed and eager that there was only pleasure and no pain. They kissed more passionately once Nigel was inside him. Philip wrapped his legs around Nigel's torso and pulled him into his body as far as possible. Nigel gasped and shed tears. Philip felt so complete and truly close to him. Their orgasms were almost simultaneous. Afterward, they went into the shower together and washed each other.

Philip said, "I want you to sleep with me. I want to hold you close to me."

Nigel said, "There is nothing in the world that I want more than this right now."

Gradually, Nigel revealed that he was from a famous banking family. His father had insisted that he learn the business from the lowliest position to the top. He had attempted to develop relationships with a few men, but ultimately they had been more interested in his money than in his well-being. Nigel was proud of Philip for struggling to have a career in something he loved. He made Philip agree that he would never question what Nigel wanted to do for him. He had enough money to do everything he wanted, and he felt like it was also Philip's money. He told Philip that he would fly to Rome every weekend in his jet, and he wanted Philip to just accept that. Philip agreed.

Philip invited Nigel to the set in London when he was shooting his important scene with Carroll. Philip was even more motivated in playing his character because he knew that Nigel was watching him. Nigel took them out to dinner afterward to celebrate. Later, Carroll told Philip that Nigel was the one for him. Philip was falling in love with him, but he was hesitant to give himself completely.

When the movie was finished, Carroll and Philip returned home to Rome. Nigel came the first weekend and told Philip he wanted to stay with him in Rome. Philip knew that he meant it, but he wanted Nigel to continue his work. Nigel agreed to go back to London during the week and return to Rome on weekends. Although Nigel offered to buy an apartment for them, Philip wanted to continue living with his American friend Robert in his walk-up apartment near the Colosseum. Nigel understood and loved sleeping with Philip in the single bed in his tiny room, which had a window box full of red-orange geraniums.

Nigel invited Philip to go to Florence to see the Henry Moore exhibition. In 1972 it was the largest collection of works by a living artist to be presented in Italy and was an honor for the British art world. Philip and Nigel took the train from Rome to Florence, a pleasant journey through Tuscany. Philip loved the hum and motion of the train and snuggled up to Nigel. When they arrived at the train station, a limousine was waiting to take them to the Grand Hotel.

Philip had come to expect luxury; it was commonplace with Nigel. But he hadn't anticipated the next move in Nigel's arsenal of surprises. When they had settled into their sumptuous suite, Nigel made a phone call. Soon there was a tap at the door, and there stood Hardy Amies and Ken Fleetwood.

Philip exclaimed, "Hi! Nigel didn't tell me you were coming. What a nice surprise!"

Amies said, "We wanted to share this experience with you two lovebirds."

Nigel interjected, "Philip doesn't know anything about what is in store for him."

Philip impulsively kissed Nigel, prompting Nigel to tell

Hardy and Ken that they would meet them for dinner at five o'clock and then go to Forte di Belvedere for the exhibit.

As soon as their friends left, Philip dragged Nigel over to the huge four-poster bed. He didn't even take time to turn down the bed but attacked Nigel on the handwoven bedspread. They kissed until they felt like fainting. Then they proceeded to what the French called *la petite mort*, "the little death"—orgasm.

Philip was looking forward to dinner at a little café and a limousine ride up the mountain to the Forte—it was the idealized Italian romantic experience.

Nigel said, "I have a present for you." He retrieved a huge box from the closet.

Philip dived into it and said, "A formal tuxedo with tails? I thought this was a casual event outdoors at the fort."

"It is," assured Nigel. "But afterward we are going to the Henry Moore reception with Hardy to see the dress he made for Princess Margaret. She is the guest of honor. Then we'll have a private supper with her. I didn't tell you because I didn't want you to worry about it."

Philip said, "I don't have the proper shoes."

Nigel said, "I know your sizes in everything and brought everything you need. They're in the box."

Philip shouted, "I love this black cashmere cape with the red lining! Can I really wear it?"

Nigel said, "Yes, you'll need it. It can get cold at night on the mountain."

They both played dress-up as they put on their formal attire. Philip had never had so much fun dressing up, especially with Nigel constantly groping him until he got an erection.

Philip protested, "We can't do it again. There's no time."

"I'm just preparing you for tonight," explained Nigel.

"What if I'm introduced to the princess with a hard-on?"

"She would love it."

The garden at Belvedere was the perfect setting for Henry Moore's massive sculptures. Chairs had been arranged around a stage, where a British master of ceremonies gave a glowing speech about the artist. When he spoke about the beautiful courtyard designed by "Michael Angello," the Italians murmured, "Che è, che è? Who is it?" Philip was used to the British pronunciation of Italian words and understood that he meant Michelangelo. When someone whispered the correct pronunciation to the speaker, only Philip and Nigel giggled.

Princess Margaret graciously received about one hundred people at the reception. Much prettier in person than in her photos, she made Philip feel disoriented. He was awkward at first, calling her "Your Highness." After they had had a few drinks, she told him to call her "ma'am, darling." She felt comfortable enough with them to talk about naughty indiscretions in the palace.

Nigel affectionately put his arm around Philip.

"You must bring our American gentleman to the palace for tea," she pronounced.

"Thank you, ma'am. I would like that."

Nigel whispered in his ear, "You made a big hit."

TWENTY-THREE

Arrivederci Roma

When Philip had visited Rome with John in 1960, they had discovered the group The American Theater. Watching their performance of *Dark of the Moon*, Philip had longed to be up on the stage, playing the witch boy who falls in love with Barbara Allen and becomes human. After the performance he and John had spoken with the actors, who had lived in Rome for several years and tried to put on at least one play a year in English. Almost all the English-speaking actors living in Rome had joined the company. Philip had immediately felt a bond with this band of artists, even though he could not join them at the time because he was still in the army.

Now, thirteen years later, Philip was in Rome to act in movies. Acting in movies was entirely different from acting on the stage. It took a different type of artistry to know how to play to the camera, to know how the smallest gesture conveyed so much, to know how to live the part even after the twenty-ninth take.

But Philip's first love was the theater, and he was overjoyed to find The American Theater still in existence and planning a night of one-act plays. For his audition he played Tom in a scene from *The Glass Menagerie* by Tennessee Williams. He was accepted into the company and was cast in the two-character play *The Loveliest Afternoon of the Year* by the American playwright John Guare. The latter portrayed a surrealistic situation between a man and a woman who meet in Central Park, and the actors had to breathe life into the characters to make them believable. During rehearsals Philip had to give a lot of support to his leading lady, Lisa, who seemed to be a wise and worldly person but who was addicted to another actor in the company and was attempting to break up with him for the tenth time. When Philip tried to find out why she had put up with so much abuse from this man, Lisa said, "His dick is the perfect size for me. It hits the right spot. If I have it regularly, I'm happy and can overlook the rest of his bad qualities."

Despite Lisa's reasoning, she was drained of all energy and dragged through rehearsals. This forced Philip to work more intensely on his character to compensate for her lack of reaction to him. He had to fall in love with her, so he focused on her beautiful red hair, which he loved to touch. This gesture created the reality of love for her onstage. His character had to tell her a preposterous story about his sister having her arm ripped off by a polar bear in the zoo in the park. When the script mentioned the Plaza Hotel, his favorite spot in New York, all Philip had to do was visualize the hotel to transfer the feelings and motivation to the scene.

On opening night, Nigel came from London and sent Philip three dozen white orchids. Nigel and Carroll and all Philip's friends in Rome attended the opening-night performance. Philip was filled with anxiety over Lisa. How was he going to have the energy to bring his character to life, along with her character? He needn't have worried. As soon as the curtain went up, Lisa sprang into action, and Philip almost fell over the park bench—which was actually in character and caused the audience to laugh. Philip became so angry at Lisa for causing him to worry that he started to compete with her energy and activity. This made the play soar—and the audience with it. At the curtain call, Philip and Lisa received a standing ovation as they hugged each other.

The actors cried backstage from great relief and the intense emotion they had felt portraying their characters. All Philip's friends were so happy that he and Lisa had done such a wonderful job, and Nigel was kissing him before Carroll could even get to him. Backstage, along with Philip's friends, was a man he had not met before—Franco Zeffirelli, the noted Italian director. Zeffirelli praised Philip for his realism in his portrayal of an unusual character and asked him to come to his office the next day: he was casting a play that he would direct in New York City.

Philip was thrilled but also fearful as he approached Zeffirelli's office. He had been elated in the past over the possibility of getting a good part with a great director, only to be disappointed when things did not work out. Would this happen with Zeffirelli too?

Zeffirelli won him over immediately with his charming manner and good looks. There was a twinkle in his eyes that could make a person feel he was the most important person in the world at that moment. And truthfully, when you auditioned for a part in Zeffirelli's plays, at that moment you were the most important person to him. He offered Philip the lead part, Saint Francis of Assisi. Philip was stunned. He had always admired Saint Francis for what he believed and the way he had lived those beliefs.

Philip had once gone to Assisi and prayed in the cave where Saint Francis had prayed. There miraculously had been a little cross woven of string and twigs in the place where Philip had chosen to kneel. In Zeffirelli's office, as Philip recalled that moment, he began to shake.

Zeffirelli put his arms around him and said, "Don't worry. I will protect your sensitivity and guide you in portraying Saint Francis."

Philip said, "I do feel safe with you. I have faith in you."

Zeffirelli said, "I will never abandon you. I sense that you have suffered great abandonment and loss. You will no longer suffer in the real world—only on the stage."

Philip replied, "Oh, that is true. I had a great love in the past, but it is over. It is partially my fault, and I tried to make up for it, but I couldn't repair the damage that had been done."

Zeffirelli said, "Saint Francis made his sacrifices for God. In the play you do not have to make your sacrifices for God, but you must have a real person that you would make a great sacrifice for. It must be for a specific person, or it will come across as false. Do you have someone that you would sacrifice everything for?"

Philip said immediately, "Yes. There is one person I would give my life for."

"Then everything you sacrifice in the play must be for that person. The audience will believe you are doing it for God."

Zeffirelli gave him a climactic scene to take home and study: Saint Francis goes to the town square to tell the people that he is no longer the son of his father, but the son of God. He takes off all his clothes and returns them to his father. He does not want anything from his earthly father. He will go naked into the woods, and the Lord will provide for him.

Zeffirelli asked Philip, "Will you be able to strip onstage

221

and be completely relaxed in front of all the townspeople and the audience?"

"If I do that part of the play for God, I'll be able to do it."

The next day, Philip auditioned for Zeffirelli and some producers. He had memorized the scene in which Francis takes off his clothes and returns them to his father and becomes the son of God. The words naturally led Philip to take off his clothes and throw them aside. Everyone was convinced that he was Saint Francis, and when his monologue was over, he casually put on his clothes again.

Philip got the part.

Soon after, he and Nigel went to New York City. Nigel rented an apartment for them on Sutton Place.

On opening night, Nigel met Philip's family and was especially gracious to his sister, Loreen, who had schizophrenia. Nigel had volunteered at Bethlem Royal Hospital in London and had learned how to interact with mental patients. Loreen thought his accent was cute, and she was very comfortable with him. A chain-smoker who normally couldn't go more than a few minutes without a cigarette, she managed to sit through the entire first act of the play. At intermission, Nigel took her outside so she could have a cigarette.

Philip's parents were amazed at their son's performance. His father told people in the lobby, "My son is Saint Francis."

There was a moment in the second act when Francis told Clare, who was in love with him, that they must dedicate their lives to God. Suddenly, Philip could not hear anything. He continued to speak and move as he had rehearsed, but he was floating in a blue mist. He believed what he said, and peace descended upon him. He felt immersed in the action of the play, while believing in the other actors. Never before had he had an experience like this in the theater or performed for an audience so enraptured and bursting with thunderous applause.

The traditional party at Sardi's after the play was a usual one filled with excitement and anticipation of the newspaper reviews. The *New York Times* of December 15, 1973, was brought in by the stage manager. He shouted that the play was a hit. Once the crowd had stopped screaming, he said, "History has been made today too. The headline of the *New York Times* says that the American Psychiatric Association has removed homosexuality from the DSM II classifications of mental disorders."

Another cheer arose as Philip kissed Nigel and said, "Yesterday we were mentally ill, but today we are cured." Philip knew he would never have another moment like this— his first opening night and now confirmation by the American Psychiatric Association that he was no longer an outcast. It was a dream come true. To complete the dream, the critics praised Philip. The play and almost all the actors received accolades.

The actress who portrayed Clare said, "Philip, I felt something strange happen when you told me to dedicate my life to God."

Philip said, "I almost blacked out. I felt like a power had taken over—and not our great director's power."

"Did I hear someone call me great?" chimed in Zeffirelli.

"Everyone has called you great," Philip said sincerely.

Soon afterward, Nigel asked Philip, "Do you want to go home?"

"Yes, please." Philip was so relieved to have such a caring person looking out for his well-being.

Philip and Nigel put Philip's family in the limousine and sent them to their hotel. Then the couple took a taxi to their apartment on Sutton Place and sat down to talk about their extraordinary evening.

TWENTY-FOUR

Having It All

Philip appreciated and enjoyed the luxury of the apartment on Sutton Place. He told Nigel about his first experience with Sutton Place.

Philip said, "When I first came to New York, I heard about Sutton Place. I couldn't imagine what it was. So one day I went to Fifty-Seventh Street by myself and walked toward the East River. At the end of the street, there was a strip of houses above East River Drive with a little park that overlooked the river. I walked by the beautiful houses, wondering which one Marilyn Monroe or Judy Garland had lived in. There were little indentations, not exactly streets but little spaces, between some of the houses. I walked past one where there was laughter coming from teenage girls in the basement kitchen. I could look down through the window at street level and see them. They were having breakfast at the kitchen table. I had not seen an apartment in New York that had an eat-in kitchen. I suddenly became afraid that they might think I was a Peeping Tom and ran off."

Nigel said, "I'm so sorry you had a deprived life, but it has made you the person that I love."

Philip hugged him and said, "Thanks to you, I now have the home I dreamed of."

Nigel replied, "I love to give you things that you enjoy. I can appreciate them through your eyes. You have brought such awareness and happiness into my life."

"I hope that I can bring you happiness through my performances," said Philip.

"I shall be there every night. I had never experienced anything like that. There was a part where I thought you were really Saint Francis talking to God. I felt chills all over my body."

"I did have a peculiar feeling during that part," confessed Philip. "I've never had that before while acting. I'm happy that my parents were here to see it and to meet you. It's been hard for them to accept that I'm gay and also an actor. But tonight they were proud of me for both—because of you and the play."

"It really was special. I wish my parents were here, but they will be able to come next week. You will still be in it?" joked Nigel.

"I'm trapped. I have to give two weeks' notice if I want to leave," joked Philip. "I'm so fortunate. I do have everything I've always wanted—Broadway, a wonderful boyfriend, and a happy family. My sister was so happy and really enjoyed herself for the first time in quite a while. You were so good with her. That means so much to me."

"I already feel a part of your family. I hope that you will have a chance to be with my family, so you can get to know them better. Princess Margaret already told them how much she likes you," said Nigel.

As they prepared for bed, Philip felt awkward. He had told

Nigel about Zeffirelli's command that Philip remain celibate during the run of the show. Philip understood the importance of being chaste so that he could convey the holiness of Saint Francis. He didn't know if Nigel, being Episcopalian, understood the significance of this or if he could also remain celibate. Philip had given him permission to have sex outside of their relationship, but Nigel had said he had no desire to do so.

Nigel said, "I have prepared the guest bedroom for me. I don't want you or me to have any temptations while sleeping together. I don't think I could keep my hands off you. I do love to be near you all the time."

"You are always near me, in my heart. No one has ever been so kind and considerate," said Philip. He hugged and kissed Nigel good night.

When Philip got into bed, he began to cry. He knew something was missing. What could it be? Maybe it was the normal letdown after opening night. Maybe it was the sudden quietness after all the chaos of the show and party. Then it hit him. It was John. He still loved John and wished he could have been here with him. He remembered telling John how he would love him forever. In light of all the happiness in his life, he knew he still missed John—and he would forever.

Philip got up and went into Nigel's room.

Nigel said, "What's the matter?"

"I have to tell you something. It wouldn't be fair to you."

"Whatever it is, we will work it out. Don't worry. Please tell me."

Philip said, "I still love John."

Nigel said, "I thought it might be that. I don't care. As long as you are with me, I can live with that. As long as I am your second love, it doesn't matter."

"It's not fair to you."

"Who knows what is fair? I only know that I have never been so happy with someone. If we could get married, I would give you half of all I have as in a heterosexual marriage. We could be bound together for life."

Philip said, "You know that will never happen. Other people will always see me as your lover, the person you have sex with."

"I would be proud to have you as my lover."

"I won't be able to live this kind of life. As long as I was striving to attain a goal, I could push aside my longing for John. Now that I have everything that I ever wanted, this longing is too painful."

Nigel said, "I'll do anything to help you. I promise I'll dedicate my life to you."

Philip said, "I know that you will. If only I had met you first. Life doesn't give us things we want at the time that we want them. I do believe that if we pray and also work hard, God will eventually give us everything. It's just not when we expect to get certain things."

"I do understand how you feel. Please tell me what I can do."

"I never told you that years ago I went to a Trappist monastery. There is one near Rochester. I went to visit a friend from high school who had joined the order. I really wanted to see what it was like because I had become disillusioned with the theater in New York. In fact, that is the reason I moved to Rome."

Nigel said, "I thought that you had come to Rome to escape something."

Philip said, "It did work for a while. When I met you, I thought I could stay in Europe forever. I often marveled at those Americans who became expatriates and loved living there."

"I would have lived anywhere with you."

"I shall always treasure that. Now you can do me a favor. Will you drive me to the monastery when it's time for me to go? When I went there before, I drove myself, so they knew that I was not ready to stay there. I spoke with a monk who told me that I could not join them there with the intention of running away from something. He said if I were going to become a monk, it would have to be because there was something drawing me there and not because I was running away from something. He also said I could not go there while thinking I was going to sacrifice my life for God. He said that my life as an actor was harder than living there as a monk. I asked him if they slept on straw mats and flogged themselves. He laughed and said that they didn't do that anymore. He said they worked on the farm and made things. That's how they support themselves. I regret that I will not be able to support my parents and sister."

Nigel said, "That is something I can do. It will give me pleasure to know I am doing something important for you. I shall support them for the rest of their lives. We have a foundation to help mentally ill people. I shall provide a life of luxury for them."

Philip said, "You are a saint. I shall pray for you until I die."

They held each other and cried.

About the Author

Patrick J. Suraci is the author of *Male Sexual Armor: Erotic Fantasies and Sexual Realities of the Cop on the Beat and the Man in the Street* and *Sybil in Her Own Words: The Untold Story of Shirley Mason, Her Multiple Personalities and Paintings.* He served in the US Army in Germany during the Berlin Crisis of 1961. He is a psychologist in Manhattan.

CPSIA information can be obtained
at www.ICGtesting.com
Printed in the USA
LVHW111448130319
610514LV00007B/38/P